T*WITCH

DEAD WRONG

H.B. GILMOUR
& RANDI REISFELD

SCHOLASTIC

NEW YORK   TORONTO   LONDON   AUCKLAND   SYDNEY
MEXICO CITY   NEW DELHI   HONG KONG   BUENOS AIRES

IF YOU PURCHASED THIS BOOK WITHOUT A COVER, YOU SHOULD BE AWARE THAT THIS BOOK IS STOLEN PROPERTY. IT WAS REPORTED AS "UNSOLD AND DESTROYED" TO THE PUBLISHER, AND NEITHER THE AUTHOR NOR THE PUBLISHER HAS RECEIVED ANY PAYMENT FOR THIS "STRIPPED BOOK."

NO PART OF THIS PUBLICATION MAY BE REPRODUCED, STORED IN A RE-TRIEVAL SYSTEM, OR TRANSMITTED IN ANY FORM OR BY ANY MEANS, ELEC-TRONIC, MECHANICAL, PHOTOCOPYING, RECORDING, OR OTHERWISE, WITHOUT WRITTEN PERMISSION OF THE PUBLISHER. FOR INFORMATION REGARDING PERMISSION, WRITE TO SCHOLASTIC INC., ATTENTION: PERMISSIONS DEPARTMENT, 557 BROADWAY, NEW YORK, NY 10012.

ISBN 0-439-24073-5

TEXT COPYRIGHT © 2002 BY H.B. GILMOUR AND RANDI REISFELD. ILLUSTRATIONS COPYRIGHT © 2001 BY SCHOLASTIC INC.

ALL RIGHTS RESERVED. PUBLISHED BY SCHOLASTIC INC.

SCHOLASTIC AND ASSOCIATED LOGOS ARE TRADEMARKS AND/OR REGISTERED TRADEMARKS OF SCHOLASTIC INC.

12 11 10 9 8 7 6 5 4   3 4 5 6 7/0

PRINTED IN THE U.S.A.
FIRST SCHOLASTIC PRINTING, APRIL 2002   40

CHAPTER ONE
A FRANTIC E-MAIL

Camryn Barnes looked up from the window seat, where she'd been doing her homework. It was just past three in the afternoon and the winter sky was already darkening. "Could you stop that? You're getting on my nerves," she called to her sister.

"Didn't know you had any," Alex snapped back. She was on the computer, the PC she shared with Cam, in the bedroom she shared with Cam, sitting on the ergonomically correct computer chair that had formerly been Cam's alone, trying to focus on a writing assignment she wished was Cam's. It wasn't that big a deal. A book report. Still, Alex was having a hard time concentrating.

"And just what am I doing that's upsetting your delicate balance?"

"Obsessing," Cam answered, adjusting the scrunchie that held her gleaming auburn hair in a ponytail.

"Excuse me?" Offended, Alex spun on the computer chair to face her so-called identical twin. At this very moment, Cam was all pink sweater set and skinny bootlegs while Alex was in wrinkled flannel and side-striped sweats. Cam was Galleria Girl, fashion forward, while Alex was content to recycle her Crow Creek, Montana, threads. Identical? She thought not. One look would tell anybody how unalike they were. And just to prove it, Alex had recently bleached her spiky short hair platinum blond with pale green streaks.

"We cannot go to Montana for winter break," Cam said. "We already have other plans."

"Yo, no trespassing," Alex said angrily. "I am sooo sorry I ever taught you how to break into my mind. And I wasn't obsessing. I was just thinking about that disgusting weasel, Ike —"

Isaac Fielding, or Ike, was the creep Alex's mom had been married to at the time of Alex's adoption. He was part of the package, just one of two toxic things that came with Sara. Like the cigarettes that had killed her, Ike was poisonous and cost way too much. He had disappeared when Alex was in grade school, taking all of

Sara's money and leaving a pile of debts she could never pay off.

Now he was back.

Now, months after Sara's death, just when Alex had finally agreed to become the legal ward of David and Emily Barnes, the trustworthy twosome who'd reared Cam. Now, when Cam's adoptive parents were in the final stages of becoming Alexandra Fielding's legal guardians.

Dave was a lawyer, Emily an interior designer. They lived in a classy neighborhood in the cutesy town of Marble Bay, Massachusetts. And they'd already filed the papers requesting guardianship. Nothing stood in their way — except, suddenly, Ike.

Drawn by the smell of money, like a rat to cheese, Ike had crept out of his hiding place and was hungry for handouts. By way of a lawyer's letter, Mr. Isaac Fielding was challenging the Barneses' petition for guardianship, claiming that he, as Alex's adoptive father, was her legal custodian.

Cam was right. Alex had been obsessing. She'd found out that Ike had recently been seen around Crow Creek. And Alex couldn't get the idea out of her head that she ought to visit her old Montana hometown and have a little chat with Daddy Dearest —

"Face it. A *chat* is so not what you're itching to

have," Cam announced, startling Alex again. "And BTW, sista, you didn't teach me how to read your mind. It's just one of the fabulous gifts and prizes I get for being your T'Witch," using their shorthand for Twin Witch. "And one that I sometimes wish I could turn off. Like tonight!" Cam rolled her eyes and sighed. "Well, could you at least hold it down? I mean, think your revenge thoughts a little more quietly. I've got a final tomorrow —"

"And I've got this dumb book report to do." Alex turned back to the computer, determined to forget about Icky Ike for now.

The minute she put him out of her mind, in came Cade.

No fair, Alex thought. She didn't want to think about Cade Richman, either. What was the use? Of course, the hottie was everything Ike wasn't — young, handsome, smart, honest, loyal, lovable. Cade, the coolest thing that had happened to Alex since she'd landed in Marble Bay, had only one thing in common with Ike. He'd left her, too.

Okay, it wasn't personal. Cade's father had moved the family to Paris two weeks ago.

Alex supposed there was some comfort in knowing that Cam was going through similar stuff. The hunk her sister was crushed on — though Cam would probably classify it as a mere "crush-ette" and think of herself as

more "like-sick" than "lovesick" — was gone, too. Shane, the young warlock who'd helped them a few weeks back, had returned to Coventry Island, home of many witches and warlocks of all ages.

Of course, Cam still had Marble Bay High's tall, dark, and handsome hottie Jason to cheer her up.

Alex glanced at her sister sitting on the window seat, focused on her book. If Cam could do it, she could, too. Forget Cade. Ditto for Ike. Alex sighed. Just concentrate on the assignment, she told herself.

She was surprisingly successful — for about five minutes, or until the computer sang out, "You've got mail."

Als, you've got to come to Montana right away! Evan is in big trouble. He's been suspended from school — and arrested! Oh, please, Alex. I don't know who else to turn to —

The message was from Lucinda. Lucinda Carmelson. Evan Fretts and Lucinda were Alex's best friends back in Montana. Correction: They were her best friends in the world!

Evan arrested? Not possible. They'd hung together through grade school and beyond — through Ike's disappearance, and Lucinda's dad getting laid off work, and Evan's mom's drinking binges. And though they didn't act cool or dress hot like most of the kids at school, Ev

and Luce were smart, decent, and honest. So what could Evan have possibly done to get suspended and arrested? What kind of "big trouble" could he have gotten into?

Alex turned to glance at Cam again. She was still curled up on the window seat. Her homework rested in her lap as she stared out at the wintry sky, frosty gray now with the threat of snow.

"Camryn," Alex called to her. "Come here. Look at this e-mail from Lucinda."

No answer.

Was Susie Sunshine being moody? She had to have heard Alex. She was just across the room. Okay, so their bedroom was big — nearly big enough to hold the dinky trailer Alex and Sara had called home after Ike split — but it wasn't so huge that Cam couldn't hear her. For some reason, Alex decided, her sister was ignoring her.

Was the girl going hormonal? That would be so unlike Cam the Perfect, Cam the Placid.

Okay, then Alex would answer Luce's 911. Without her twin's input. We'll be there, she wrote back. We have a long weekend coming up. We'll come the day after tomorrow.

With an uneasy glance at Cam, Alex double-clicked SEND. Her e-mail vanished into cyberspace, speeding to the Crow Creek Public Library, where Lucinda's message had originated.

"I told Lucinda we'd go to Montana on our break," Alex tried again.

But Cam was still gazing out the window. Looking clueless. And cold.

As Alex watched, her sister began to shiver. She hugged herself and rocked back and forth, her eyes unfocused, looking inward.

"Cam?" Alex called tentatively. "Cami, what are you staring at?" Suddenly, Alex realized what was happening. "What are you seeing?" she whispered. But it was useless to question Cam when she was in this state. Clearly, she was having a vision — one of the vivid, visual premonitions she'd had all her life.

Cam's sight — like Alex's hearing and sense of smell — was honed, hyper, over-the-top. While Alex could hear a leaf drop miles away, Cam could see it. She could also picture the leaf plummeting before it took the plunge — sometimes minutes before, sometimes days. Alex could move things — just by imagining that leaf lodging in someone's hair, she could make it stick there. And Cam's combustible eyes could light it up.

What was Sister Sizzler seeing now?

"Your friend," Cam said now in a hoarse, spooky voice. She wasn't fully "awake" yet. "The boy from Montana. Evan. He's in trouble."

"Give me news, not history," Alex said. "That's

why I told Lucinda we'd be going to Crow Creek for the break."

"That's why you what?!" Cam was wide awake now, wincing from the post-premonition headache she usually had after a vision. "We can't go to Montana!"

"Tell me about it," Alex said. "Your vision, I mean. What did you see?"

"Evan. I think." Cam closed her eyes, remembering. She had met Evan only once. "He looked different, but I got this vibe that it was him. He was someplace cold and familiar. It was a weird place that we'd been to before. But it looked empty, except for Evan and two other boys. There was a woman with them, too. A big woman dressed in black. She was shivering and crying." Cam shuddered at the memory. "The boys were bad, Alex. I mean, there was a darkness around them, an inky aura. They were trying to hand Evan this . . . this . . . red container. I don't know what it was. Something dangerous. One of them, with, like, bad teeth and this evil grin, was saying, 'You got to. It's too late now.' And Evan kept pushing whatever it was away, going, 'No. No way, man. No.'"

"And then what happened?" Alex urged.

"Then someone said, 'Cami, what are you staring at?'"

"Um, that was me," Alex confessed.

"Double duh." Cam rolled her extraordinary gray eyes. "And speaking of no way. No way are we going to

Crow Creek. We've already got plans. We're going to Brianna's birthday bash. Her dad's flying in from L.A. and throwing this monster blowout for her. And he's rented a whole floor in one of the best hotels in Boston, so we can all hang together —"

Brianna Waxman was one of Cam's best friends. Brianna's father, Alex had heard, was this big-shot movie producer. He was always breaking promises to Bree, backing out of their plans, and having his assistants handle his daughter's personal phone calls and requests.

"Well, yeah." Cam was back in the mind-reading business. "He's canceled on every appointment he's ever made with Bree. I hope he doesn't bail on this one. Not now."

Alex made a face. "Whatever. Bree only invited *me* because you made her."

"Big whoop. We have to stick together, don't we?"

"Do we?" Alex asked skeptically.

"Hello," Cam said, lifting her gold sun charm and zipping it back and forth on its delicate chain.

Automatically, Alex clutched its mate, the half-moon necklace she was wearing.

Both charms had been made by their blood father, Aron, a brilliant young warlock who'd supposedly been murdered by his brother Thantos the day Alex and Cam were born.

Nothing weird about us, though, Alex thought. Just your basic identical twins who were separated at birth to prevent their evil uncle from continuing his killing spree.

"We need to stick together," Cam said again. "Our mojo, our magick, is stronger when we do, and way stronger when the necklaces connect."

"So that's why you wanted me along?" Alex raised an eyebrow at her twin. "Why not just take my moon charm? It would be way cheaper for Brianna's rich daddy."

"That's not the only reason —" Cam protested.

"Well, I'm not going," Alex announced. "And neither are you. We're witches, remember? We're supposed to help those in trouble. And that does not include those in trouble because they have only two hands and twelve shopping bags like Brianna Waxman."

Cam frowned. "Lose the sarcasm, Alex. Something's going on with her — something bad. I don't know what it is exactly, but I can sense it. I just have this feeling that disappointing her is not what we want to do right now."

"So we have to spend our break trailing after Bree and watching her max out her daddy's credit cards? Cam, listen." Alex shifted gears from sarcastic to serious. "My creepy stepdad — the one who's fighting your folks in court, the slimeball who could ruin our chances of staying together — is probably back in Crow Creek."

Cam reconsidered. She'd never before imagined Ike winning — or considered the consequences.

"You said we had to stick together," Alex reminded her. "Well, one, if Ike Fielding wins his court case, we won't be able to. And two, I'm definitely going to Montana. Not just to help Evan, who's been my true-blue bud since grade school, but to find out what Ike really wants — which is not now and has never been me. I've got to change his mind . . . by any means necessary," Alex added pointedly.

"Including witchcraft." Cam got the point.

"Times two," Alex said.

Say yes. Do it, Cam thought to herself, remembering how even her best friend, Beth Fish, let alone Bree, could never in a million years understand how it felt to know you were radically different from every other kid you knew. Until, one day, you met someone who not only looked exactly like you, but knew, firsthand, what you felt, thought, feared, and were.

"Okay, I want to go with you," Cam acknowledged. "I'm in. But they'll never let us —"

"Who, Emily and Dave?"

Cam nodded. She was still uneasy about calling her parents — or at least the couple she had believed for fourteen years were her bio'rents — by their first names.

"They will." Alex's gray eyes glinted with mischief.

"Trust me. When I'm done, they'll *insist* we go to Montana."

"Oh, no. You're scheming and scrambling your thoughts so I can't possibly read and reject them. What are you going to do?" Cam demanded. "Tell me!"

"I just have to check out one little thing with Mrs. Bass at the Crow Creek Library," Alex said, turning back to the computer. "You know her."

"Only through e-mail," Cam reminded her sister. "What's she got to do with it?"

"Well, who do you think Emily and Dave would rather have us spend the break with — Eric Waxman, a Hollywood producer who showed up at the Academy Awards with a starlet dressed in spray-on graffiti, or Doris Bass, my surrogate mother, a mature, highly respected, small-town librarian?"

"Duh," said Cam. "Can I poll the audience?"

CHAPTER TWO
TWO FOR MONTANA

"Gosh, I'm really looking forward to going to Boston," Alex said at supper that night.

"Gosh!" Dylan, Cam's "little" brother — the child (nearly six feet tall now) whom Emily had given birth to less than a year after Cam's adoption — almost choked on a brussels sprout. He'd been spitting sprouts into his napkin throughout the meal. Now, thanks to Alex, he'd just actually swallowed one. Appalled, Dylan shook his head, and the small gold rings he wore on one earlobe sparkled through his shaggy, blue-streaked blond hair.

Ignoring him, Alex continued. "In honor of Bree's birthday, her dad said we can do anything we want all week. He'll be way too busy to chaperone us."

Emily looked pointedly at Dave, who shrugged, as surprised as she was.

"Where'd you hear that?" Cam asked, a forkful of gummy mashed potatoes halted inches from her mouth. "Ouch!"

"Sorry," Alex said. "I was swinging my foot. Did I get you?"

"What exactly did he mean by that?" Emily asked.

"Well, Mr. Waxman's got a new girlfriend," Alex filled them in. "Two, actually —"

"Sick," Dylan said admiringly.

Emily shook her blond head. "Two girlfriends?"

Dave laughed. His thick droopy mustache seemed to chortle with him.

"And he's got tons of work to do," Alex added, "so we'll be on our own pretty much —"

"I don't think so." Emily threw her husband a si-lencing look.

"Oh, except for the movie guys like Ben and Josh and Brice he promised to introduce us to —"

Emily was not amused.

"Don't worry," Cam added mischievously. "Bree's dad never does what he says. He's totally undependable." At least that part was true.

"David?" Emily challenged.

"Uh, maybe you could go with them?" he suggested.

"You know I can't. I've got two deadlines coming up." Cam's mom was trying to get a country house redecorated before spring and working on an all-weather porch for a home in the Heights. She was a much better interior designer than a cook. "What about you?"

Dave's dark curls bounced as he shook his head. "The Blake case is going to trial next week —"

"Don't ask me," Dylan teased. "Robbie Meeks's family is taking us boarding at Stratton —"

"You know what I'd really rather do?" It was time to introduce the alternative, Alex decided. "I mean, dating movie stars and making the Boston club scene sounds fresh, but I'd so love to go visit Mrs. Bass, the librarian at Crow Creek. She was my mom's best friend —"

"You want to spend your vacation with a librarian?" Dave sounded skeptical.

"But Alex," Cam said, playing along, "she's such an *old* lady, and so strict. Of course, I haven't met her, except through her e-mails to Alex," she told Dave and Emily again, "but she sounds so . . . straitlaced."

"Oh, she is," Alex agreed. "Straitlaced and sensible. I haven't been back there in over six months. Haven't visited my mom's — I mean, Sara's — grave or seen my old friends —"

"Of course, there's not much to do in Crow Creek, except for that Big Sky theme park." Cam groused.

"Which closes for the winter," Alex added.

"Nothing to do but read." Cam sighed. "I mean, I guess we could give old Mrs. Bass a hand at the library —"

"Won't Bree be disappointed if you change plans at the last minute?" Emily asked.

"Like she'd notice?" Alex said. "Everyone else is going to be there."

"She *will* notice," Cam interrupted, feeling more guilty than she let on, "but we'll do something to make up for it when we get back."

"Okay," Dave said, with a trace of impatience in his usually jovial voice. "What's really going on?"

Alex quickly shoveled a forkful of mystery meat into her mouth while Cam, as see-through as J. Lo's designer duds, said, "That is so not fair. We were just —"

Dave did a talk-to-the-hand stop sign. "You want to go to Montana," he said. "You want us to trust you, right? You'll have to trust us, then."

"Nailed!" Dylan grinned.

When all else fails, try the truth, Cam silently advised her twin.

Alex shot her an evil look. *Hello*, she said silently to her sister, *if they know it's to change Ike's mind, Dave will have a gazillion legal reasons why we should stay out of it; and if I tell them we want to help a friend of mine who's in "big trouble," Emily'll freak —*

Hello, Cam reminded her, *they're on to us. Under the circumstances, some of the truth's better than none! Now, you want to do it or should I?*

Alex took a breath and put down her fork — which was no hardship, considering how vomitacious Emily's cuisine was. Finally, she said, "I want to go home. Just once, before you become my legal guardians —"

"If that awful man has his way we may not even be able to —" Emily began.

Alex shivered. Ike had found out where she was and, without writing or phoning or trying to get in touch with her personally, he'd hired a lawyer, claiming that he wanted Alex back.

Not gonna happen. NGH! Alex heard Cam assure her. And she needed the assurance. She needed Cam. The thought of living with Ike Fielding again . . .

Cam took Alex's hand under the table.

We've got to get there — but how? Alex asked.

Get the 'rents to finance our trip, Cam answered.

Brilliant, Alex scoffed silently. *Planning to mug them?*

Sort of, Cam shot back. *Emotionally.*

She hated to do this. Actually, she wasn't even sure it would work. But Cam aimed a searing stare at Alex, carefully holding back so that her twin's eyes would sting but not burn.

It worked. Not only did Alex start to cry, but she squeezed Cam's hand so hard, Cam got misty-eyed, too.

"Alex? Are you okay?" Dave put his hand on her shoulder.

"Camryn?" Emily sounded alarmed.

Not knowing where her tears had come from, Alex saw through blurry eyes that Cam was crying, too.

"I've got some money," Cam blubbered. "The money Grandma put away for me. I'll pay for the tickets."

"I'm going," Alex asserted. "I want to. I need to. Just once. Once before you guys become my guardians, I want to go back. I need to . . . say good-bye to Sara. To my mom. I miss her so much. I need to really say good-bye. And see my friends again. And the places we used to go." She was sniffling back tears for real now.

For a moment, there was silence.

Alex heard Cam thinking, *OMG, the girl is good. She's a total Gwyneth!*

Finally, Dave cleared his throat. "We'll work it out," he said, looking at his wife.

"Of course," Emily answered.

CHAPTER THREE
COVENTRY

Ileana felt it, smelled it — fear.

Like an electric current, it ran up her spine. It stung her nostrils, left a sour metal taste in her mouth.

Terror.

Only it wasn't *her* emotion. It was someone else's. Far away.

Whatever you want. I'll call it off. I'll tell the lawyers to leave them alone. Just . . . don't hurt me anymore. My arm! Please, whoever you are, whatever you are, don't kill me!

"Ileana?" Karsh's cry brought the beautiful young witch back . . . to the overwarm cottage, the pleasant crackle of the fire in the hearth, the green scent of the herbs she was chopping.

"Are you all right?" he called from his sickbed.

Ileana tossed her head, flipping back a cascade of pale blond curls. "Of course," she answered, with her back to him. "I'm perfectly well. You're the one who needs help."

But the awful feeling clung to her. The feeling — no, the certainty — that something bad was about to happen. Or had already occurred. Something evil.

Well, what of it? What had it to do with her? She had her plans.

Ileana refused to turn around to face Karsh.

It didn't matter. The wily old warlock could read her like a book.

She was like a good mystery, Karsh had always thought, one that could be read over and over again and counted on, each time, to deliver new delights and surprises.

Ileana was often bad-tempered, yet she could stun one with sudden kindness. Wildly self-centered, she would risk her life doing what she believed to be right. She was very outspoken — her words sharp as swords — yet it was hard for her to say what she really meant. And hardly ever what she felt.

Though Ileana had never met them, had no idea

who they were, the child Karsh had reared had inherited the different natures of her father and mother.

From his sickbed, he studied her now. Tall, flaxen-haired, wrapped in her long velvet cape and elegant winter boots, Ileana was preparing herbs for his midday medication.

"Haven't you anything better to do," she grumbled, "than stare at my back? Are you afraid I'll mix up your potions and poison you? You know I can't — not until you tell me where I came from and how you came to be my guardian. Which I think you'd be grateful enough to do by now."

Weeks ago, Karsh had been kidnapped. It was Ileana who'd risked all to rescue him. Now, she was nursing him back to health.

Karsh rubbed his head and hid a smile. His once-thick curls had thinned to a nappy white fuzz — like a favorite plush toy rubbed bare by a child. "My dear witch —"

"Call me goddess," Ileana snapped, as he should have known she would.

"Goddess, then. My well-being is of no great consequence. It is the twins we must protect," Karsh continued. "As their magick grows stronger, so does their desire to protect and help others —"

"And as their desire to protect and help others grows," Ileana complained, "so does their recklessness."

"Indeed," Karsh teased her, "they are very much like their guardian."

Fifteen years ago, on the day the twins were born, their father was murdered and their mother disappeared.

No one had understood why Karsh urged the Coventry Island Unity Council to appoint Ileana, then a teenager herself, the twins' guardian. The entire coven had thought Karsh was crazy to put the infants' welfare in the hands of one so immature and irresponsible. But Karsh was Ileana's guardian. And he'd promised the Council he'd guide her in the awesome task — though, even then, he'd had faith in Ileana's talent and goodness.

And, indeed, together they had kept the extraordinary little witches alive — against great odds. Their uncle Lord Thantos had been searching for the girls ever since the day he killed their father. It was Karsh and Ileana who separated the twins, sending one to be reared in Montana, the other to Massachusetts, where they now both lived in the charming seaside town of Marble Bay.

Ileana carried the potion to him. "Look at you," she clucked mournfully as he took the herbs she'd mixed. "You're skin and bones. If only that madman had given you your tonic. If only I'd saved you sooner. If only I'd been there when you were taken by his moronic brother —"

She was speaking of the twins' hateful uncles, Lord Thantos and his foul-smelling brother, Fredo. They had kidnapped Karsh in yet another attempt to capture the twins.

Suddenly, the terrible sureness that something evil was happening assaulted Ileana again. But it was happening far away, she thought. Nowhere near Coventry Island and her beloved, bedridden guardian. But was it near the twins? Were Alexandra and Camryn in harm's way?

Once more, the terrorized voice intruded on her thoughts. She listened to it begging for mercy. Scrambling on its haunches across a carpetless floor. Nails clawing, boots scraping, as it propelled itself inside an echoing metal container. A railroad boxcar? No, something stationary, without wheels. Something that sat run-down and isolated in a snowbound field.

Who was it? Where was it coming from? A frozen place with vast mountains and big sky. It could be anywhere.

Except Marble Bay, she realized with relief. There was no hint of salt water, no cawing of seabirds.

Confident that the girls were safe, Ileana turned to face Karsh. "Brice! Yes, Brice Stanley, the warlock movie star. I was supposed to visit him in California weeks ago. Big mistake! Naturally, I had to hustle off to Massachusetts to save our trouble-prone little witches. Then I had to single-handedly rescue you from that kidnapping mess."

"I'm sorry to have inconvenienced you," Karsh sighed. "Why don't you visit your friend Brice now?" he suggested. "Lord Grivveness or Lady Rhianna can stop by to prepare my herbs and —"

"That is precisely what I plan to do!" Ileana announced. "Lady Rhianna, indeed!" she muttered. "That plump old dumpling of a witch can't take care of you. Not the way I do."

Karsh tried not to grin.

"Anyway, I'm not going to California," Ileana huffed. "I can't —"

"Why?" Karsh asked anxiously. "Are the twins in trouble again?"

"No. Because Brice isn't there. He's making a movie in Mexico! It has nothing to do with our dear little T'Witches."

"T'Witches?"

"Oh, didn't you know?" Ileana asked. "That's what they call themselves. Twins. Witches. T'Witches."

"How clever." Karsh grinned.

"They are certainly that. Too clever, if you ask me," Ileana allowed. "Which, I know, you didn't." She sighed theatrically. "Well, at least you won't have to worry about them for a while. For a change — a very refreshing change — they're safe and settled in Marble Bay."

CHAPTER FOUR
THE HOMECOMING

"There she is, Pop, in the red sweater! Get out, she let her hair go natural!" Lucinda's shriek rose above the bustle of the airport noise. The grinning girl with the Raggedy Ann hairdo pushed through the crowd, hauling her father behind her. "No, *there's* Alex, the platinum blond in the black peacoat!"

Pushing past two businessmen exchanging cards, Lucinda flung herself into Alex's arms. "It's you, Als!"

Lucinda, chunky with flawless pale skin and the sweetest dimpled grin. The last time Alex had seen her — months ago, last summer — Luce had been wearing her hair in a torrent of skinny braids, some of which she'd dyed red. The braids were undone now, but the dye was brighter than ever — a beautiful blazing black-rooted orange.

Alex inhaled Lucinda's special scent, the sweet, clean smell of baby powder. Evan's scent, she remembered, was a rich dark chocolate fragrance. And Sara's had been green and fresh as new-mown grass. For an awful moment, Alex thought she might cry. Instead, she teased Luce. "Sorry, I'm Camryn Barnes. And who might you be?"

The real Cam was warily looking around the airport, focusing on men in suits and boots — pointy-toed cowboy boots, round-toed black motorcycle boots, mahogany dress boots — and women in big hair and shiny exercise suits.

Snob much? Alex silently ragged her.

Luce took one look at Cam's open mouth and laughed. "No way, José," she said, turning back to Alex. "You're my true-blue BFF."

While they hugged, Lucinda's dad pumped Cam's hand with his huge callused paw. Then, Mr. Carmelson hugged Alex and Lucinda shook Cam's hand. "I'm so psyched. I can't believe you came!"

"Where's Ev?" Craning to see beyond Mr. Carmelson's billboard-sized shoulders, Alex scanned the crowd, looking for her bud, with his high, wide cheekbones, tawny complexion, and wild, frizzy dreadlocks.

Evan Fretts had been their rock, hers and Luce's, their protector, and their designated driver from the day his mama, blasted on Wild Turkey, tossed him the keys to her rusty pickup and wished him happy birthday — two weeks after the fact.

Evan's mama drank too much. And cried a lot. And sometimes disappeared for days. But you couldn't say a word against her. Not while Evan was around. He loved her to pieces. That was how he was. The more of a basket case you were, the more you could depend on him. So where was he now? "He hasn't been arrested again, has he?" Alex asked anxiously.

"Nope, it's just, um, I didn't tell him you were coming," Lucinda admitted sheepishly. "I wanted to fill you in first. Let's grab a Coke or something and talk while Pop takes your stuff to the car."

Alex allowed Luce to lead her through the small but busy airport. Cam lagged behind. Aside from feeling like a gawking tourist, Bree-guilt had been nagging at her since they'd left Massachusetts. Cam could still hear Bree's rant ringing in her ears.

"So I'm hearing you say you can't make my gala 'cause you and identwin have elsewhere to be. Of course, trailing Clone Girl to be-it-ever-so-humble, her no-place-like-home is so more important than my fifteenth birthday," Brianna had sniped.

The words were Bree's, the snide, pretend snobbery, but the emotions behind them betrayed real hurt. Cam's sense that something was really off the hook bad in Bree's world was stronger than ever. Cam pondered. Brianna *had* lost some weight lately, but that didn't mean anything. Bree tended to bounce up and down — and besides, she was on this new exercise kick.

Lucinda's hearty laughter brought Cam back to the present. "You were at a rave?! Get out! Oh, wow, you guys, I'm so glad you're here."

"Parts of us are," Alex said, glancing back at her slowpoke sister. "Take Camryn, for instance. Her body's here, but her brain's back in Marble Bay."

Just tune in anytime, Cam silently retorted, annoyed that Alex had trespassed on her thoughts. *My privacy is so a thing of the past.* Aloud, she added, "I was thinking about Brianna. We've got to find her a totally outrageous birthday gift."

"No prob," Alex promised.

"As if. Bree's so picky. What are we going to get in Crow Creek? There's no one remotely like her out here."

"And that would be . . . a bad thing?" Alex teased as they stepped into the airport's fast-food stall.

Lucinda looked from one to the other of them. "You guys." She giggled, shaking her head. "You're still scrapping. Just like when you first met."

They grabbed an empty table on which the last customer had left a Styrofoam coffee cup and a couple of packets of sugar, most of it spilled.

Cam raised an eyebrow at the mess, but sat down. She'd met both Luce and Ev the same day she'd seen Alex for the first time. The three of them had been working at Big Sky, the frontier theme park that the Barnes family — vacationing in Montana — had decided to check out. Luce remembered right. Their first encounter had not been pretty. Cam had been so shocked at seeing her face peering out from under Alex's punk-gelled, blue-streaked hair, she'd gone into a whirlwind of sarcasm and denial.

"So what's up with Evan?" Cam asked, changing the subject.

"Is Ike still around?" Alex asked at the same time.

"Easy one first. I don't know about Ike," Luce confessed. "I checked around. Mrs. Bass saw him at the cemetery, you know . . . at your mom's grave," Luce said delicately. "And Pop heard there was someone hanging around your old trailer. That dog-ugly landlord of yours, Hardy Beeson, couldn't rent the place, I heard. Too cheap to fix it up. But no new Ike sightings."

Alex nodded. "Okay. Now, about Evan —"

Lucinda sighed, making circles in the spilled sugar. "His mom's drinking got really, really bad. She started up again just before you left, remember?"

Alex did. She remembered that after Sara's funeral they'd talked about what Alex would do next. Evan had wished she could stay at his place for a while, only his mother's drinking had gotten out of hand —

"Anyway, first you took off, then Evan's daddy left for Coeur d'Alene, in Idaho, looking for work. So Ev was left with his ma. And she started showing up at school totally loaded and just embarrassing him. So, naturally, kids started in on him, teasing him, making fun of her."

"Oh, no. That must've driven Ev wild," Alex noted.

"Totally," Luce said. "They were, like, saying her Indian name was Firewater Fretts or Wild Turkey," she explained to them. "You know Ev," Lucinda said to Alex. "He had to fight every single one of them — so he got suspended for a while."

"And?" Alex had started picking at the Styrofoam cup, which seemed to be grossing out Cam.

Do you even know who drank from that? she heard her sister ask.

Gee, and I thought Emily was staying home, Alex silently responded.

Oblivious, Lucinda rolled on. "So then he started taking up kung fu or whatever." She rolled her eyes again. "He really bites at it, a total no-belt. And when we went back in September, he was different, Als. He was real an-

gry and no fun anymore. I mean, he started avoiding me toward the end of the summer, and by the time school started up again, he'd stopped joking around, never teased or kidded me anymore. And also, and this is the bad part, he started hanging out with Riggs and Kyle Applebee and Derek Jasper —"

"Snakes and stooges?!" Alex exclaimed. That was what she, Luce, and Evan used to call the trio — and it was Evan who'd come up with the name! Snakes and stooges, 'cause there were three of them acting stupid as the Three Stooges, and as mean as snakes. Plus, the Applebee brothers wore ratty snakeskin boots to school all the time, and they and their crony Derek Jasper — who wore a ten-gallon hat with a big old feather in the hatband — all had rattlesnake tattoos around their upper arms.

"Hanging with the stooges is dumb, but it's not a crime. How did Ev get arrested?" Alex asked.

"Someone left a threatening note in a teacher's mailbox — Mr. Adamson, the gym teacher, you remember him?" Luce answered. "I don't know for sure, but kids started saying it was a death threat. And since, like the day before, Adamson was riding Ev in gym about his bad attitude and what a wuss he was at martial arts, everyone immediately assumed he wrote the note. Then a kid said he saw a knife in Evan's locker — and the principal looked and, sure enough, there was one. Which, of course, Evan said he'd never seen before —"

"Was it his?" Cam asked.

"Not that I know. I never saw it but I believed Evan. The principal didn't. So the police got called and hauled Ev off to jail and he was in there for a couple of nights but they had to let him go. But he got suspended from school again and they're probably going to kick him out permanently and —" *Should I tell them the rest?*

Alex was about to say, "Of course you should," when she realized that Luce hadn't asked the question aloud.

"And?" Cam prompted. Lucinda had stopped abruptly. Too abruptly.

Should I mention Evan's warning? I said I wouldn't. Maybe I got it wrong. I could have misunderstood. . . . Alex listened as Luce wrestled with her conscience. The girl was stressing.

Say something, say something, tell us! Alex wished Luce could hear her. But Lucinda couldn't — and left the rest unsaid. Alex decided not to push her — yet.

CHAPTER FIVE
THE HOLLOW

Lucinda's dad dropped Alex and Cam at Mrs. Bass's house. As Mr. Carmelson's rusty wreck drove away, the twins went to the rear of the house, where the heat-fogged kitchen windows and the smell of warm food told them that Sara's old friend was at home.

They were welcomed with hugs and homemade macaroni and cheese by the tall, slim, attractive woman in jeans and a sweatshirt, who Cam had characterized as old and straitlaced.

"I've got to get back to work soon," Doris Bass told them apologetically. "Ben's traveling this week but he sends regards." Ben was Doris's husband of twenty years, a book salesman for a New York publishing company.

"Just stash your stuff upstairs. There's only one guest room, but it's got two beds and an old black-and-white TV. Make yourselves at home and I'll be back around five."

There wasn't much time to quiz Mrs. Bass about Ike. During lunch, she told them she'd been over to the cemetery sometime around the holidays. She'd brought a pretty wreath she'd made. It hadn't snowed all that much — but enough to see footprints leading right to Sara's grave — made by someone wearing pointy-toed boots. Mrs. Bass's heart had fallen the minute she'd noticed them. Isaac, she'd immediately thought. He'd always worn these ugly pointy-toed boots with two-inch heels to make him look taller and feel important.

And, sure enough, there'd been someone standing there, a man in a parka and cowboy hat staring down at the stone. You had to walk around a stand of evergreens to get to the gravesite and, by the time Mrs. Bass emerged from the trees, the man was gone. But it was Isaac, she knew. The heartless dope had left a pair of dice on the grave. Dice! Who but Isaac Fielding would've done a darn dumb thing like that? His idea of sentimental, she guessed.

They went upstairs and unpacked shortly after Mrs. Bass left. "Did you notice Lucinda freaking?" Alex asked. Cam shook her head, and her sister filled her in. "She

didn't tell us everything. There's something about some warning Evan gave her. . . . She was afraid to talk about it —"

"Why don't we go over to Evan's, find out from him what's going on?" Cam suggested.

"Def idea. You got a snowmobile? They live over in the hollow, about ten miles from here — and we've got no wheels or skis —"

"Maybe he'd come over here. We could phone —"

"If their phone's still working. When Mrs. Fretts goes on a bender, everything gets shut off sooner or later. Telephone, electric . . . At least they've got a wood stove to keep the place warm."

Cam flopped down on the twin bed nearest the window. "I'm tired . . . and out of ideas —"

"That was fast," Alex teased. "World record, I think. Okay, wheels, wheels, wheels. We need someone with four-wheel drive and a license."

Cam said nothing, but gazed out the window. "Is it cold in here?" she asked after a moment, shuddering. She sounded distant, distracted.

Alex stopped pacing, fell back onto the second bed, and studied her sister. The sudden weariness, the chill . . . Cam's black-rimmed gray eyes seemed unfocused, as if she were looking inward, not at the silent snowfall outside.

Finally, Cam asked slowly, dreamily, "Als . . . do you know anyone about five-ten, with brown, I think, hair kind of curling out of a black knit cap? A boy with black eyes and a dimple in his chin?"

"Crooked smile, with a classic little space between his two front teeth? Andy Yatz," Alex answered, astounded.

"Who's that?" Cam blinked, then winced and covered her eyes.

"This guy I went to Crow Creek Regional with. But I never mentioned him to you —"

"He's going to" — the phone rang — "call," Cam finished.

"Mojo girl," Alex exclaimed, leaping up. "You are such the sibyl, seer, and psychic!"

Her twin's excited shout made Cam flinch again. "Chill," she ordered as Alex flew out the door and thundered down the stairs to answer the phone. "How unfair is it?" Cam called weakly after her. "I get the headache, you get the phone call from the hottie."

For a second, a split but stellar second, Cam had thought the smiling boy she'd seen in her premonition was Shane. She sighed. Just weeks ago, the teen warlock who had been sent by their hulking uncle Thantos to snare them had switched sides. He'd gone from being the

twins' enemy to their ally; from serving Thantos to saving Cam's gullible best friend, Beth.

Cam wondered what Shane was doing now, back on Coventry Island. She wondered whether she'd ever see him again. . . .

"It was Andy!" Alex was back three minutes and two aspirin later. "He's home from college and heard I was in town. He's coming right over. Said sure he'd drop us at the Fretts place, but he won't hang around if Ev is there," she told Cam, who was resting her forehead against the icy windowpane, staring out at a gale of snow blowing off bare, wind-swirled trees.

Shane. Alex caught Cam's melancholy vibe.

"Don't," her sister warned her, without turning around.

"I was just going to say I hope we see him again," Alex explained.

"If he's still alive," Cam said. "He crossed our vengeful uncle, remember? So . . . you were saying?"

"Actually, Andy was saying" — Alex crossed to the window and casually stroked her sister's hair, which, if the situation had been reversed, Alex would totally have hated — "that he heard Evan's really changed a lot and kind of doesn't like anyone anymore. If Ev's not around, though, Andy'll drive us back."

Despite her headache, Cam was pleased that — like Alex's gifts — the hunches and premonitions her Marble Bay buds called "Cam's mojo" worked this far from home. She'd never heard anything about Andy Yatz before and suddenly she'd seen this hunk-a-rama in a red plaid lumberjack shirt and black knit cap dialing a telephone number and grinning like mad.

It wasn't Shane but, as boys in visions went, this one was way cooler than the scary glimpse she'd had of Evan and his skanky, tattooed friends.

Andy Yatz drove up in an old Chevy station wagon. Alex saw him from the guest-room window. Rifling through her suitcase for her black turtleneck sweater, she hollered down to Cam to get the door. Which Cam did, a second before Andy rang the bell.

"Hey," he exclaimed, taking in the auburn-haired, gray-eyed girl in the red sweater and clingy black ski pants. "You look fantastic. Life out East agrees with you."

Cam laughed. "It must. I've lived there forever."

Andy, in his plaid shirt and black cap, looked exactly as he had in her vision. He was studying her now, trying to figure out what she'd meant.

"I'm not Alex," Cam finally said. "She'll be down in a minute. I'm Camryn, her sister."

Andy tugged off his cap. His head looked like a top-

ographical map, jungles of tangled curls interspersed with damp flatlands of hat hair. But his dark eyes sparkled and the space between his front teeth was, as Alex had said, classic.

"I heard she had a sister . . . but no one said —"

"That we were twins?" Alex was suddenly at Cam's side, looking fine and foxy in her black sweater and jeans.

Andy's grin widened. And Cam felt a hint of jealousy as he looked Alex over with obvious joy. "I couldn't believe it when I heard you were back. Are you staying?"

"For a couple of days," Alex said. She cocked her head and frowned unexpectedly. "Anyway, thanks for coming by and giving us a lift —"

Cam was surprised at the sudden coolness in her sister's voice. "What's up?" she asked as they followed Andy to his car.

"He's got the hots for someone," Alex reported. "He was checking us out but thinking of *her* —"

"Bumosity," Cam groaned. "He is such the rural babe. Who's the lucky girl?"

Alex shrugged and they took off, three of them in the roomy front seat, with Cam in the middle. There was no need for mind reading on the ride to Evan's. The twins peppered Andy with questions — beginning with Alex's blurted, "So are you, like, seeing someone?"

"Huh?" Andy was startled.

"Um, I think Lucinda mentioned it," Cam bailed out her sister.

"Lucinda? Lucinda Carmelson?" Andy asked, as if Luce were ice cream, his favorite flavor. "She thinks I'm seeing someone — is that what she said? No way. How'd she say it? I mean, you know, like she cared?"

"Lucinda?" Cam and Alex stared at the boy, taken aback. *Holy cow, he's into Luce*, Alex thought.

Duh, Cam responded silently. They glanced at each other, then broke up laughing.

"Yeah, yeah —" Andy blushed, then started laughing, too. "Hey, I always liked her," he confessed. "And, I don't know, on my trips home from school she's looking really fine lately —"

"I second that emotion." Alex let the embarrassed hottie off the hook and moved on to the bonus round. Evan.

Andy knew, as everyone did, that Evan had bonded with the rattlesnake crew. From what he'd heard *they'd* put Alex's bud up to bad-mouthing Mr. Adamson, who Derek Jasper had a grudge against. Andy doubted that Evan wrote the threatening note — even though Adamson was supposed to have made fun of his cruddy karate performance. But then someone had seen the knife. Seen it tumble out of Evan's locker when the principal pried it

open. "He's not like you remember him, Alex," Andy cautioned again. "He's really changed."

Evan's house was out of town, up a snowplowed, two-lane mountain road and then down a narrow, pitted dirt path. Almost every two miles, a mailbox would appear. The fourth box was an old rusty one labeled FRETTS. Judging by what was left of the paint chips on the container, it had once been red, white, and blue.

"That's it," Alex said, excited just to see Ev's last name on the run-down mailbox.

While Andy waited in the car, Cam trailed her sister along a path made by tire ruts in frozen mud. Carefully stepping over a piece of crusty inner tube and then a discarded hubcap, Cam shook her head involuntarily. How could someone who looked so like her, who knew her inner thoughts and feelings, be so pumped to be back in this awful place?

There was nothing remotely Marble Bay about the peeling mailbox or the small, one-story shack at the end of the tacky trail. Leaning away from the wind, the house's wooden frame was worn to an ashy gray. Unbelievably, in the gusting snow, a woman was hanging wash on a line tied between two porch posts.

"Mrs. Fretts?" Alex called softly, clearly happy to see Ev's mom, even though the alcohol fumes drifting from her were making Alex slightly dizzy.

The woman was wrapped in a brown army blanket, from the bottom of which a flowered housecoat fluttered. A hunting cap with dangling earflaps and unbuckled rubber galoshes completed her outfit.

"Mrs. Fretts," Alex called again, louder.

Evan's mom turned and looked over the twins' heads, as if the voice she'd heard had called to her from the clouds.

"Is she blind?" Cam whispered.

"More like blind drunk," Alex said. "Hey, Mrs. Fretts! Remember me? It's Alex. Alex Fielding, Sara's daughter."

"She's not here!" the woman roared at the sky. "Now get! Scoot! Quit hollering at me!"

"Maybe we should go," Cam urged. "Come back later or tomorrow when she's —"

"Is Evan here?" Alex ignored her sister. "I'm here to see Evan!" she shouted through cold, cupped hands.

Finally, Mrs. Fretts brought them into focus. Instantly, she dropped her clothespin bag and the frozen-stiff wrinkled shirt she'd been about to hang. Through swollen squinting eyes, she stared in disbelief at Alex and Camryn. "I'm seeing double! And she's not even dressed the same! Evan, help! Come quick!"

The weaving woman grabbed onto the porch post to steady herself and, as if she'd become suddenly tired, slid down the pillar to the rickety wooden floor.

Alex hurried to her. "Mrs. Fretts, I'm sorry. We didn't mean to scare you. It's just me, Alex — and this is my sister, Cam. You're not seeing things. She's real and she's my twin." She reached out to help her friend's mother, but Mrs. Fretts slapped at her hands and began to screech piercingly.

Freaked, Cam could barely keep from screaming herself.

Suddenly, the front door banged open and there was Evan, boiling mad. In two strides, he was standing over Alex, with a shotgun pointed at her head. "What's going on? What'd you do to my mama?"

Alex looked up. "Ev. Evan, it's Alex! Put that stupid thing away!"

Cam peeked out from between her hands and saw a boy aiming a shotgun at her sister. It was Evan — looking nothing like the teasing, easygoing guy with the bushy, blond-tinged dreadlocks she'd met less than a year ago. Grim, breathing hard, battling panic and rage, it was the Evan she had seen in her vision!

But the porch he was standing on now was not where she'd pictured him. This scene was crisp, clear, free of the strange, shadowy shapes that had loomed behind him in her dream. . . .

Cam's eyes widened and, almost on their own, telescoped in on the muzzle of the gun. It was cheap metal, she saw. Aluminum or tin. Easy to heat, even in this weather. Before she realized that the weapon Evan was holding was a toy, the metal turned red and then white; smoke curled from the muzzle and the barrel began to bend.

A little boy charged outside, followed by an eight- or nine-year-old girl. "You give me back my gun," the little boy howled at Evan.

"Nicky, get back in the house," the girl scolded.

They both saw the twisted toy at the same time and gasped.

"Alex?!" Evan came to his senses, looked at the bent-barreled gun, and started laughing out loud. "Alex Fielding," he sputtered.

Alex jumped up, punched Evan's arm, and pointed at Cam. "You remember my look-alike from the Ferris wheel at Big Sky? She's weirder than me by a mile, bro."

"Little trick I picked up in first-year toy bending," Cam joked nervously. "I'm a magic major."

"Honor student, I bet." Evan handed the toy back to his crestfallen little brother. "It was broken before," he tried to explain to the boy. "I told you it was just a cheap toy. I'll get you another one, a better one this time." His sister helped their mother to her feet, then walked her and the snuffling little boy back into the house. Evan

shook his head happily at Alex. "Yo, dudess. So how's life in the sneeze state?"

"Sneeze state?" Cam asked.

"Yeah, Mass-ah, ah, ahchoo-zits!" Evan teased.

The wild and wooly blond dreads Alex had loved so much were now tightly cornrowed flat against his head. The ratty overalls and sneakers he'd always worn had been replaced by tight black jeans, stomping boots, and a black hooded sweatshirt, the back of which someone had painted a skeleton in a top hat, identified in gothic letters as "Dr. Death."

"Yo, nasty boy, we've got to talk —" Alex said.

"I'm down with that," Ev answered.

"About you and snakes and stooges."

Evan's grin faded fast. His face grew hard. The muscles in his cheeks rippled and his dark eyes flashed a warning glare. Then as swiftly as his anger came, it vanished. He lightened up. "Later for that," he said. "When'd you get here? Back to Crow Creek, I mean? Are you back for good?"

"Just for a week. We're staying in town, at Mrs. Bass's. Can you give us a lift back there?" Alex asked, remembering Andy waiting in his car.

"Sure thing," Ev said. "Be out in a minute." While he went inside to check on his mother, Cam hurried out to

the road to thank Andy and tell him they had a ride home.

Alex sat down on the porch, her back against the bottom of the post, her legs tented, arms wrapped around her knees. As Lucinda and Andy had warned, Evan was different — his hair, his clothes, his quick, menacing anger.

Most of all, Evan's scent had changed. His sweet chocolate fragrance had taken on a burnt edge. Alex's nostrils still held the scorched tang, the bitter aftertaste she'd first sampled when her friend had burst out onto the porch with a shotgun aimed at her head.

CHAPTER SIX
THE CEMETERY

It was barely morning. A thin gray light edged the curtains in Mrs. Bass's guest room. Sleep was impossible for Cam. Instead she found herself reviewing yesterday. Evan's mom, sick, barely able to stand, clutching the porch pillar for balance. The wailing children, frightened by what Cam had done to the toy gun. Stopping at Lucinda's place so Alex could say hi to Mrs. Carmelson. Evan hadn't wanted to bother Luce. "She doesn't need me messing up her life," he'd said mysteriously, but Alex had insisted on going by.

How different Luce's house had been from Evan's. It was as small and gray as his, but full of laughter and life. And hugs! Everyone from Luce's three-year-old niece to her eighty-three-year-old grandmother had welcomed Cam as though they'd known her forever. Which, in a sense, they had — they'd known her "spitting image," the other "pea in the pod," Alex.

With so much love freely given away, it was a wonder Lucinda had any left over for Andy Yatz. But she plainly did. When Alex mentioned that Andy had given them a lift, she'd blushed, shrugged, and changed the subject. But Alex caught her thinking, *Andy is* so *fine!* She'd forwarded Luce's thoughts to her twin just as Evan laughed and said, "Yo, Luce is wickedly crushed out on candy Andy Yatz."

Then, as quickly as he'd turned into laughing boy, Evan had become somber and angry again. Angry, or ashamed, Cam couldn't tell which. He'd just snapped his mouth shut, frowned, and looked down at his boots.

"Ev, what's up?" Alex had demanded.

"Nothing," he'd insisted. "I just want to get out of here. I mean, nothing personal, Luce, but it's just better all around if you don't hang with me."

Alex had wanted to visit Sara's grave before going back to Mrs. Bass's house, but it was snowing too hard by then. If it let up that night, Evan promised, he'd take them over to the cemetery in the morning.

Well, it was morning. Cam cuddled under the quilt,

remembering now that she'd had some kind of whack dream — about a place. She and someone, maybe Alex, had been hiding someplace where strange dinosaur-tall silhouettes loomed through a mist. It was, Cam thought, the same place she'd seen Evan and the two other boys in the scary vision she'd had back home. . . .

"What time is it?" The muffled voice came from Alex, who'd put a pillow over her head. "Is it still snowing?"

"Seven-thirty," Cam answered, craning her neck to see out the window. "It's still dark out, but I don't see any snow falling —"

Alex scrambled out of bed and looked out the window for herself. "It stopped. We can go to the cemetery . . . and I also want to go out to the trailer."

Though she was warm in her bed, Cam shivered.

Alex, who'd just turned toward her sister, noticed. "What's up?" she asked. "What did you see?"

"Someone who looks just like me," Cam said in a spooky voice. "Only her hair's the color of peroxide; and she's wearing boxer shorts and a tee —"

Alex whisked the pillow from her bed and hurled it at her sister. "Get up and don't go weird on me, okay? You looked like you were, you know, shaking."

"Actually, Als, I didn't *see* anything exactly —" Cam

hugged the pillow her sister had tossed and tried to explain. "But I did get this yucky, kind of bummed-out feeling when you mentioned the trailer."

"Duh, that's because it's a yucky, bummed-out place, one of the major landmarks on the Crow Creek historical tour of dorky dwellings and heinous tin homes."

By the time they showered, dressed, and gobbled half of the amazing hotcakes Mrs. Bass had fixed, Evan arrived and began beeping for them from the driveway. "For goodness' sake, it's too early for such a racket. Tell him to come in. There's plenty for everyone," the librarian insisted on her way out of the kitchen to get ready for work.

Alex ran outside to the back porch and hollered for Evan to come in; Cam threw open the kitchen window and seconded the invite. But Evan stayed stubbornly where he was, in the cab of his rusty pickup, blowing on his bare hands and acting like he hadn't heard them.

"You ought to harvest those potatoes," Alex grumbled at him, ten minutes later, as she climbed into the truck.

"Potatoes?"

"Yes, the ones growing in your ears," Alex snapped. "You heard us calling you, didn't you?"

"Yeah," Evan conceded, pulling out of the driveway. "You still want to go over to the cemetery, right?"

Alex softened. "I do, thanks. So what was up back there? Why wouldn't you come inside? Why'd you play deaf?"

He shrugged and suddenly Alex heard him thinking, *Yo, that's all Mrs. B needs — me in her house. She's better off not even knowing me. Not the way things are. Not the way it's gonna go down. I don't want to bring her grief.*

Alex sent her twin a mental message. *Evan's buggin' over something that's about to happen, something seriously bad —*

Cam suddenly realized, *I bet it's happening at Big Sky.* Big Sky — that was it, the misty place she'd seen in her vision. The massive, menacing shapes were just the winter-empty Ferris wheel and roller coaster framed against a snowbound sky.

"Big Sky?" Alex blurted.

Evan hit the brakes. The pickup stalled and skidded sideways along the icy road, jarring the girls hard against their seat belts. "What are you talking about?" he demanded, once he'd gotten the truck under control again.

"You trying to kill us?" Alex yelled at him.

"What about 'Big Sky'?" he hollered back at her. "What's going on? What do you know about it?!"

"You tell us," Alex demanded. "You and Luce — my so-called best buds — suddenly everyone's got all these serious deep secrets. No one's leveling with me. No one's telling the whole truth about anything —"

Evan started up the motor again. It coughed and sputtered, but he stayed silent.

"Evan!" Alex prodded him. "Don't shut me out. We've known each other forever, known, trusted, backed up —"

"Leave it alone, Als. Quit doggin' me," he ordered. "I'm not shuttin' anything. I'm trying to protect you, that's all."

"From what?" Alex wanted to know.

"From me," Evan said.

He wouldn't explain. His mind was closed on the subject. Literally! The only chain of thought Alex could break into was Evan fretting about her mentioning Big Sky. He wondered if Lucinda had let it slip. Then he remembered that he hadn't told Luce anything about what they were going to do at the park —

"Evan, you've got to trust someone," Alex whispered to him.

"I trust you," he said. "That's not the problem. Don't you get it? It's me I don't trust."

Evan pulled up to the cemetery and stopped the truck.

Alex climbed out. "We'll be right back," she told Evan, and he drove off to park.

Alex and Cam trudged up the hill to the stand of evergreens that Mrs. Bass had described.

Then Alex saw Sara's grave. Tears she didn't know she'd been hiding stung her eyes and filled her frosty nose.

Cam put an arm around her, but Alex shrugged her off. "I'm okay," she said almost angrily. "Leave me alone. Just for a couple of minutes."

Cam nodded and waited near the trees, stamping her feet and rubbing her hands together for warmth, while Alex trudged through the snow toward the little headstone.

Feeling a whirlwind of emotion, she knelt beside the grave. The tears burning her cheeks were not as surprising as the awful rush of anger she felt. She was thankful that the dice Mrs. Bass had seen were gone, but she couldn't help picturing them there, picturing Ike — whose lies, disappearance, and debts had, Alex was convinced, hurried Sara's death. Yes, yes, cigarettes had been the real culprits, but would Sara have smoked as much if Ike hadn't gambled away their house; if she hadn't been constantly worrying and working to feed and shelter her daughter while paying back the people her husband had cheated?

Now Ike wanted to mess up Alex's life. Now he was scheming to shake down Dave and Emily Barnes or take

Alex away from them and from the sister she'd finally found.

A shadow fell across Sara's grave. Cam had come up quietly behind Alex and put a comforting hand on her shoulder.

"We've got to find Ike — and stop him," Alex said without looking up.

Cam knelt beside her. "We will. I promise we'll —" She stopped abruptly and stared at the mound of snow in front of Sara's headstone.

"What is it?" Alex demanded. "What do you see? Is it the stupid dice Ike left?" she guessed, alarmed. "Leave them alone, Cam. It gets me sick to think of him being here —"

"No," her twin whispered in a soft, sleepy voice. "It's not the dice . . ." The snow she was staring at melted. A wet circle grew in the powdery frost. At its bottom, all Alex could see was a section of frozen earth.

Cam's fiery eyes stayed focused on the ice-webbed soil, heating it delicately. Under the mud, a seed stirred, then broke through the dirt. A furled stem opened its bright green leaves and purple buds began to blossom.

"Violets," Alex breathed, awestruck. "They were her favorite flower." Overcome, she pressed her tear-streaked face into the snow, into the earth her torch-eyed twin

had thawed, and inhaled the scent of fragile violets, the fragrance of Sara.

It started to snow again. Cam helped Alex up. "We'd better go," she said gently.

Alex nodded. She didn't trust herself to speak. Instead, as they made their way back to Evan's pickup, she squeezed her sister's cold, bare hand and allowed herself to lean on Cam — which Cam understood was Alex's way of expressing her gratitude and her love.

CHAPTER SEVEN
TROUBLE AT THE TRAILER

"The trailer?" Evan asked as they climbed back into his truck.

"The stream," Alex said, making a decision that surprised her as much as it did Cam. Evan shrugged and put the pickup in gear.

"I thought you wanted to see if Ike's been staying at your old place," Cam said.

"I do. But first you've got to see this stream. It's magical, Cam. I mean, it's beautiful and calming." Alex snuffled back her tears and Ev handed her a beat-up roll of paper towels he fished from the floor of the cab. She tore off a brittle, water-stained sheet and gratefully blew her nose in it. "Sara used to take us there, right, Ev? When we were kids. We used to love it so much, and she did, too. Before I face that butt-ugly trailer again, and maybe that creepy loser who's calling himself my dad, I don't know, I just thought maybe it'd be nice to sit by the stream awhile."

Cam hiked up the collar of her red jacket and said, "Brrrr. In this snow?"

"You're losing it," Evan said. "This is not your basic water-watching weather, Als."

"Ever been there in the winter?" Alex asked slyly.

"You know I haven't," Evan reminded her and — five minutes later, as they picked their way through the snowy woods to the stream — he rubbed his arms, which were prickled with goose bumps under the sleeves of his Dr. Death sweatshirt. "Yo, Als, is this place still haunted?" he tried to joke.

Alex nodded solemnly.

"Get out! It is not." Evan laughed. "You used to sucker me in all the time with that baloney, but I know better now —"

Alex parted the branches of a towering evergreen. It was like parting a prickly green curtain. Behind it a strange mist became visible, a warm heavy vapor rising off the water — which, amazingly, was gurgling and running even though the temperature was below freezing. Then Cam noticed that there was no snow alongside the stream. The bank was covered with rich green moss, tall reeds, cattails, and herbs.

Evan's eyes bugged out.

"What is this place?" Cam asked in a hushed voice.

"One of the streams that feed Crow Creek," Alex answered. She bent down and plucked a sprig of mint from the ground. Staring at it, she wondered what had made her choose it. "Mom and I used to come here in the dead of winter," she said, rubbing the spicy herb between her palms. "It was our secret place . . . the way that old tree in the park in Marble Bay is yours —"

"It *is* haunted," Cam ventured. "I can feel things . . . things swirling in the mist . . . spirits —"

That was all Evan needed. "I am so outta here!" he declared and, turning on his heels, he started back toward his pickup.

"There are spirits here," Alex said, tucking the fresh mint into her pocket and brushing off her hands. "I can hear them, but I can't make out what they're saying. I never could. It's not English. It's a different language. . . . Very old."

Impulsively, she raised her arms. Over the noise of Evan tromping through woods and the strangely soothing rush of the stream, she called out, "Ancient spirits, guide us. Be with us. Help us to help our troubled

friend." Then she laughed and shook her head. "Evan's right. I am losing it."

"No," Cam whispered. "I felt something just now. I mean, when you asked for help."

"Yeah, right." Alex sighed as they started back to the truck. "Cami, how are we going to help Evan if he won't tell us anything?"

"Well, let's see," her sister said, as if prepping for a homework assignment. "What do we know now? He's in big trouble. He told Lucinda something about it but she won't tell us. An ugly event is scheduled and Evan's in the middle of it. Oh, yeah. And he doesn't want to get anyone else involved — like Lucinda's family and Mrs. Bass. Is that about it?"

Alex nodded. "I need to get him alone. I need to convince him to talk to me. Or to *think* about what he doesn't want to tell me, so I can read his mind."

"We're pretty alone here," Cam pointed out.

"Only until we climb back into the pickup and Ev starts making small talk and concentrating on the road again."

"Maybe the car won't start or something. Then we'd be stuck here awhile with nothing to do, nowhere to go —"

"Dream on," Alex advised as they walked out of the

snowy woods and saw that Evan was already in the truck, warming it up, waiting for them.

"Your ride sounds terrible," Cam said when they reached him.

"Get out! This baby purrs," he said defensively.

"Cam's right." Alex backed her twin, though the pickup sounded like its usual clunky, coughing self. "There must be something wrong."

"Open it up," Cam challenged. "Let's have a look."

Evan shook his head at them, but climbed out and pried open the rusty hood. Cam glanced in at the engine, then focused hard on the radiator, her gray eyes going misty with concentration.

"Whoops," Alex said as a plume of black smoke erupted from the engine.

Dejected, Evan leaned against the cab of his pickup as Cam, with a thumbs-up to her twin, climbed inside.

Sticking her cold hands into the pockets of her pea jacket, Alex felt the crumbled herb. She brought it out and held it up to her nose.

"What's that?" Evan asked.

"Mint. It's good for cooling things off —" Alex had no idea how she knew that — or even whether it was true. The words had just popped out of her mouth. It sounded good, she thought.

"Maybe we should toss it into the engine," Evan said.

"It's not for cars, it's for cooling down hot emotions." Half expecting him to push her hand away, Alex held the herb under Evan's nose. "I think," she added. "Raging feelings. You know, like anger, stubbornness —"

Evan sniffed the herb. "Smells like gum," he said. "You know, spearmint." Then he laughed at himself. "Oh, right. It's mint."

"Ev," Alex asked softly, "how did a knife get into your locker?"

He didn't blink or balk. "DJ stuck it in there," he answered. "But no one believed that. Except some teacher saw him. I mean, she couldn't identify who it was, but she was sure it wasn't me. Derek's taller than I am, plus I was still wearing my dreads back then. Anyway, that's why they let me out —"

"Why did he do it?" she asked.

"Just to prove he could. Said he could get anything past security. You know Derek Jasper. Dude wears the big cowboy hat."

"Friend of the Applebees, right?"

"Flunky of the 'Bees," Evan said sourly. "They got no friends."

"What about you? Aren't they your pals now?" Alex

watched the snow clouds overhead, afraid to look at her old bud, afraid that Evan would stop talking at any moment.

"No way," he said. "They're pure mean. Every nasty bone in their bodies. Yo, I used to feel sorry for them — remember?" He turned to look at the open hood. Smoke still drifted from the motor.

"Ev, how'd you get involved with them?" Alex asked cautiously.

"How do you step into quicksand?" he answered, walking over to check out the engine.

"Was it your mom? I mean, because kids were making fun of her?"

Evan nodded. "Yeah, I guess that started it. Remember when Mrs. Applebee bailed? Kyle and Riggs know what it's like to have kids in school make fun of your mom. So they helped me out — at first. Funny," he said, without smiling. "My ma got me in with them. Now she's why I can't get out."

Alex was confused. "Your mom's involved?"

"Involved?" Now it was Evan's turn to look away. He studied the engine. "Not exactly. She's . . . aw, man. She's like . . . a hostage . . . like something they can hold over my head —"

"They wouldn't hurt her?" Alex asked, alarmed.

"Not if I go along," Evan answered.

"Go along with what?"

Evan turned to face her, but couldn't look in her eyes. He bent his head, kicked at the slush near his front tire. "You're going back, aren't you?" he asked. "I mean, you and her, your sister, you know, Cam. You two are heading out of here real soon, aren't you?"

"We're leaving early Sunday morning," Alex told him.

"Good," he said. "You don't want to be around here Sunday afternoon."

"Ev, why? What happens then?"

He looked up at her and grinned sadly. "You're back East. That's what happens."

"No, what happens here? School starts on Monday, doesn't it? Evan, what's going to happen the day before school starts again?"

"I'm going to miss you, Als." He inhaled, then blew out a big breath. "Okay, she's cooled off enough now. Hop in. Let's hit that tin toilet you used to call home — and flush out your bad stepdad."

When they got to Alex and Sara's old place, Evan decided he'd stay outside and keep an eye out for anyone who showed up.

"Okay thanks," Alex told Evan. "If you see anything suspicious, lean on that horn, okay?"

"You got it," Ev promised.

"So, did he open up?" Cam whispered as she and Alex slogged through knee-high snow toward the ramshackle mobile home.

"Yes and no," Alex answered. "He talked. He really seemed to want to. But not about what's actually going down. Except that it's slated for Sunday afternoon, the day before school starts."

"And right after we're gone," Cam said.

The trailer door was padlocked. As they drew closer, Cam saw that the bolt was hanging open. Someone had broken into the place. Alex removed the lock and slowly pulled open the door. The squeal of metal echoed through the silent woods.

Cam grabbed her sister's hand. Alex gasped and turned toward her. "What?!" she whispered. "What did you see?"

"Nothing. I just want us to go inside together."

"Okay, then, let's go —" Alex found the cement block that had served as a step up to the trailer buried in snow. She and Cam kicked it clean, then, holding hands, stepped up and through the door.

It was dark and cold inside. The thick, dusty old wooden blinds were shut. Icy air and flakes of snow blew through the cramped kitchen area. Before Alex's eyes grew accustomed to the gloom, Cam pointed to the hole in the floor through which the snowflakes were

swirling. For a moment, the cold air held down a strange and awful odor coming from the rear of the trailer.

Alex smelled it first. Gagging, she reached for the cord and flipped open the blinds. There were rags and newspapers piled up in the kitchen and an oily puddle on the floor, kerosene or turpentine, something that smelled like fuel. That was the first smell that assailed them. The second was stronger and far worse.

"Oh, no," Cam said. Wrinkling her nose at the pungent stench, she pointed toward what had once been Alex's room. "There's something over there. On the floor."

Alex followed her sister's gaze. The accordion-pleated door to her room was pulled back. An odd form, oblong and twisted, lay halfway in the room and halfway out in the narrow hallway. It looked like a rolled-up rug or a mound of rags. But Alex knew: It was a body.

Cam took a step forward and tripped over something in her path. Alex caught her as she stumbled forward, almost tumbling onto the smelly heap. Cam screamed, startling Alex, who shrieked, too.

Shaking, they both looked down at once and saw a boot — a pointy-toed boot with a two-inch heel. With trembling fingers, Alex lifted it up, just as Cam stared at the ghastly warped bundle on the floor.

She could see through the wrapping. Her knees

went weak. She grabbed Alex's arm to keep from buckling. "It's . . . a person . . . a man," Cam croaked, her mouth dry, her stomach starting to heave.

Alex's heart was pumping so hard and fast she could hardly hear herself speak. "Is it him?" she asked. "Is it Ike?" And as Cam covered her mouth to keep from hurling, Alex remembered that her twin had no idea what Isaac Fielding looked like.

Alex couldn't see through the soiled, smelly rags. It was their shape that told her a body was hidden within them. And the odor that poured from the filthy package . . . the smell . . . It wasn't Ike's. Ike's stench was the stale sour odor of all-night poker games, of sweat, fear, and mucky ashtrays in airless rooms.

This odor, this awful stinging smell was familiar and rank as spoiled cheese. It was huge . . . and not human.

Cam's eyes were tearing, her chest was heaving. "Als," she managed to whisper, "let's get out of here."

"ASAP," her sister agreed. Shrieking, they rushed for the door and, holding hands, leaped through it into the snow.

The boot flew from Alex's hand and plunked into a powdery drift in the woods. Cam started toward it but Alex stopped her. "Leave it," she said. "I know whose it is."

"Thantos?" Cam asked, shivering. "Or . . . the smell, that disgusting stink . . . was it Fredo's boot?"

"It's Ike's," Alex said, nausea welling in her throat. "It was his boot. Let's call the police."

"No way," Evan balked, when they climbed back into his pickup. "No cops. I've got enough problems —"

While the pickup flew over bumps and bounced through road craters, and Alex held her stomach and tried to keep her hotcakes down, Cam pulled out her cell phone and dialed 911. She barely had time to blurt out what they'd found in the trailer, when Evan reached across, took the phone, and clicked it off.

"They're going to want to know how you got out here, and you're going to say me, and they're going to come around asking a bunch of questions I haven't got answers to —"

Despite Cam's demands and Alex's coaxing, Evan wouldn't stop, talk, or return the cell phone until they got to Mrs. Bass's house. Then he let them out, tossed the slim-line to Cam, and sped away.

The house was empty. Mrs. Bass wasn't home from work yet. "The smell," Alex said, curling up on the living room sofa and pulling a pillow against her. "I know it's gross, but I kind of recognized it." Chilled — as much from the stench and sights in the trailer as from the cold — she kept her jacket on.

Shivering, Cam plopped down into the armchair.

"The only one I ever met who smelled that rank was Uncle Fredo," she said, glancing wishfully at the fireplace. If there had been wood in it, she thought, she might have tried to light it with a look. "You know, when he turned himself into that reeking, eight-hundred-pound lizard."

"Fredo." Alex made a face. "Another nut on our dysfunctional family tree."

"Another psycho uncle," Cam agreed.

The only good thing about the skinny, goat-bearded warlock — which was who Fredo actually was when he wasn't doing his lizard thing — was that he was as dim as a refrigerator bulb.

"So," Alex asked, "do you think Uncle Fredo's on the scene again — morphed into a lifeless bundle of rags?"

"Well, his smell is," Cam responded. "Are you sure that boot I tripped over belonged to your faux father?"

"Gotta say" — Alex hugged the pillow more tightly — "that my first thought was Thantos."

"Mine, too," Cam agreed. "But the boot's too small."

"Correctamundo," Alex tried to joke, then felt her nausea rising again. "So then I thought maybe some homeless person or one of Ev's new crew had broken into the place," she continued more somberly.

"Only Evan's pals wear snakeskin boots, no?" Cam's eyes were tearing. She wiped them away.

"Yes. But when I really got a look at the skuzzy

thing, at the worn high heels, it came down to just one self-centered bloodsucker —"

"Icky Ike?"

Alex nodded. "It was his boot, for sure —"

And disgusting, Cam thought. *The boot was peeling and smelly and old and the heel was worn down. And the trailer — how could anyone have lived in a place like that? How could her own sister, her twin, have spent fifteen minutes in that tin coffin, let alone fourteen years?*

"— but not necessarily his body," Alex was saying. "Anyone could have wandered into that place."

"That place," Cam echoed, distracted by a heinous possibility. *What if she had been the twin given to Sara, and Alex had been brought to Dave and Emily? Could she have survived? Would she even have wanted to?*

"Doubtful, your lowness," Alex said angrily.

"You were listening in?" Cam accused.

They were glaring at each other when the front door opened, and Mrs. Bass called out to them. She sounded unusually breathless.

With effort, they turned from each other. "We're right here," Alex answered, standing. But the librarian bustled in before the twins could go out to meet her.

"Sit down," she said, pulling off her ski cap and shaking the snow from it into the empty fireplace.

"Please," she added. "I mean, you don't have to sit down, I just thought you might want to, Alex."

Cam knew what Mrs. Bass was going to say. She looked at her sister, then back at Mrs. Bass.

"There's a dead man in your trailer," the librarian blurted out. "Oh, that is not how I planned to break the news. Someone called the police today and gave them an anonymous tip. A woman or a girl, the new sheriff said. Anyway, he went out to the trailer and found him. A dead man. Just dead. No blood, no signs of a struggle, no weapons —"

"When will they be able to identify who it is? Was there anything . . . distinctive about him?" Cam asked.

"Well, actually," Doris Bass remembered, "Sheriff Carson said the man had an odd patch of greenish eczema on one arm. And his nails — on that arm — were, well, long and yellow, like talons, he said. Isn't that curious?"

OMG, it was *Fredo!* Cam said telepathically to Alex. *The smell, the claws, the green lizard skin . . .*

You think he was waiting for us at the trailer? That he knew we'd show up there? Alex silently responded.

Could be, her sister said.

And then what, when we didn't get there early

enough, he died of disappointment? Maybe it was Ike. . . .

Mrs. Bass looked from one to the other of them, her eyes scrunched up inquiringly. "You're very quiet," she noted. "I didn't mean to horrify you. I . . . well, actually, I thought you might have a guess about who'd break into the trailer. I actually thought it might be Isaac Fielding — but a man that vain would never let himself go like that."

"Not a clue," Alex said quickly.

"Nu-uh," Cam agreed.

She noticed their jackets, the puddle forming around Cam's boots. "I came home as soon as I could," she said. "Did you . . . get over to . . . the cemetery?"

"We did," Cam said.

"Actually, we —" Alex began, trying to get past the idea that their toxic uncle Fredo was dead . . . dead in the trailer where Alex and her mother had lived. It didn't make sense. But nothing much made sense anymore — not since she and Cam had hooked up. Could Fredo have gone to the trailer to wait for them? But how had he died? And what was Ike Fielding's boot doing in there? Ike couldn't possibly have killed Fredo.

"Evan came by, we went to the cemetery and then up to the stream," Cam covered for her suddenly silent sister.

"Sara's stream?" Mrs. Bass sighed. "She loved that place ever since we were girls. Used to go up there to 'think' . . . meditate, they call it now. Sara heard voices up there —"

That got Alex's attention. "Get out," she exclaimed, falling back into Crow Creek slang, into Lucinda-speak. "I mean," she said, when Mrs. Bass looked at her oddly, "did she really or are you teasing us?"

"The truth? No one believed her but me. I knew she didn't lie. And I knew she wasn't crazy — even if she did fall for that fast-talking, strutting little bantam, Isaac. Biggest mistake of her life." Mrs. Bass shook her head sympathetically.

"The voices," Cam prompted.

"Yes, well, that stream, that area, was supposed to be sacred to the Crow Indians —"

"What language did they speak?" Alex asked.

"Siouan, I believe," Mrs. Bass answered, studying Alex curiously. "It's the language of the Hidatsa Crow of South Dakota. As for the stream, it's said that a revered shaman died there. A shaman is a healer; white people called them medicine men. . . ."

Doris Bass had gone full-tilt librarian on them. "Did Sara understand Siouan?" Cam interrupted.

"I don't think so, but I don't actually know. There was so much about Sara I didn't truly know. For instance,

she was psychic, I guess you could say. Very, very intuitive. She used to dabble in the paranormal. Was quite good at it, too. Which I didn't know about until we were out of college. She lost interest in it after she adopted you — oh!" Mrs. Bass suddenly remembered, "Not only is the stream a sacred Indian site, it's also the place where Sara received you, Alex — from a white-haired man she'd met at a magic convention."

Alex and Cam gasped in tandem. The white-haired man was Karsh.

CHAPTER EIGHT
THE DARK SIDE OF COVENTRY

The northern tip of Coventry Island was craggy with cliffs. Here, trees were twisted by the wind and weathered by the great lake. At the highest point of this bleak land stood Crailmore, a deserted fortress built during a time of deadly witch-hunts.

The ancestral estate of the DuBaer family — who claimed kinship to Cleopatra's physician, Merlin, Incan high priests, Polynesian chieftains, native shamans, and scores of feared and revered gurus, seers, sibyls, healers, clairvoyants, mystics, and diviners — Crailmore was where Thantos stayed (some would say "hid") when he visited his island birthplace. And it was here that his hot-headed brother, Fredo, lived.

Although the fortress could house an army, Thantos's followers — the torchbearers who had joined his angry search for his infant nieces fifteen years before — had all but deserted him. Only a handful remained, a horde of fortune-seeking fledglings, young witches and warlocks hoping to prove their daring in his reckless service. The young warlock Shane had trained here, until he'd become infatuated with one of Thantos's young nieces.

Today, however, at Thantos's command, the brothers were alone. Fredo, tugging at the wisps of hair sprouting from his pointed chin, cowered nervously in the armchair beside the fireplace — which held more cobwebs than wood. Towering above Fredo, the robustly black-bearded Thantos ground his teeth, trying to control his anger. "Three times you have failed me," he hissed. "I sent you to lure Aron's daughters — to attract them, entice them. And what did you do?"

Fredo shrugged sullenly.

"I asked you a question!" Thantos roared, lifting the silver cane he'd been using since the accident. Then he cleared his throat, even more enraged now that he'd lost his temper. "You turned yourself into a stinking lizard."

"The odor isn't my fault," Fredo argued. "It was your

bright idea. And I wish you'd remove the smell spell." He giggled suddenly, pleased with himself. "That's pretty funny — smell spell."

Thantos made a disgusted face. His hands reached forward automatically, as if he was going to grab his brother's skinny neck. Instead, he turned away, his velvet cape flaring, and began to hobble back and forth in front of Fredo. His good foot, in its hobnail boot, and his cane clacked heavily on the stone floor of the great room.

"The odor was your punishment for failing me the first time. I will undo it when you bring me Artemis and Apolla —"

"Who?" Fredo asked.

"Alexandra and Camryn, dunce! You are an embarrassment. Which is why I order you never again to shape-shift into that demented lizard —"

"It wasn't my fault I fell on you. It was an accident. And your hip is practically all healed —"

"Fredo," Thantos whispered dangerously, "listen to me. I taught you how to shape-shift. Without me — despite the reknown of our family — you'd still be a lowly apprentice trying to pass your warlock initiation rites. I taught you and now I have taken back my gift! Do you hear me? Never, never again are you to unfurl those dragon wings or wrap yourself in that putrid, scaly skin —"

"I didn't!" Fredo cried. "I did what you said. I found him in the trailer. And I didn't transform myself —"

"If ever you disobey this command, you are finished, my brother —"

Fredo gulped. "Finished?"

"I must have obedience," Thantos ranted, slashing the air with his cane. "Total, unquestioning obedience. This is a time of exceptional opportunity. You will not destroy it for me. Karsh is ill. I saw it when we held him hostage. He can't last long. And his charming companion, Ileana, a beauty like her mother —"

"And talented, like her father." Fredo smiled his yellow-toothed smile.

Thantos aimed a silencing glare at him. "Once the elder is gone, she will do my bidding —"

"You know what I don't get?" Fredo ventured carelessly. "What the big deal is about these twins. I mean, if you wanted kids, you could have had more of your own." He ducked as Thantos's cane soared toward his head. "Okay, okay," Fredo whined, his hands protectively raised. "Sorry I mentioned it!"

Thantos composed himself. Leaning against the fireplace mantle, he looked up at the full-length portrait of his mother, once the most powerful leader of the Coventry clan. She had urged him to marry but had ridiculed his choice — Beatrice, an extraordinary girl from an ordinary

family. That was the problem. As bright and beautiful as Beatrice was, her roots were undistinguished. Except for one ancestor who, scheduled to be burned at the stake, had cast a spell on her executioner who then refused to light the fire; and another who'd survived the dunking chair in Salem and lived to a ripe old age as one of the first women doctors in New England — there was barely an important witch amongst them.

But Thantos had been young and besotted and on the rebound. His one true love, after all, had married another. So he allowed himself to be smitten by the girl's golden good looks and by her strangely aristocratic, at times even arrogant, manner. He approved of the way she valued herself — as though not having a grand and powerful bloodline was more a flaw of fate than a fault of hers. And so he'd married her against his mother's caution — and lived to regret it when she died in childbirth a year later.

"Yes, Ileana will do my bidding." Still staring at the painting of his disapproving, willful mother, Thantos continued, "Because I know what she wants. *Who* she wants. I've known him since he was a boy. His name was Bevin then, a reckless orphan in my service. I took him in when he had nothing, was nobody, a forlorn little warlock. He has a new name now. Brice. He is famous, rich, and powerful. And he knows what he owes me!"

CHAPTER NINE
SNAKES AND STOOGES

The diner wasn't really crowded, it just sounded that way to Alex. At one end of the smoky restaurant, she, Cam, Lucinda, and Evan were wedged into a corner booth. Andy Yatz was a couple of tables away, sipping the dregs of a Coke and mooning over Lucinda. At the counter, an elderly twosome was noisily sharing a meat loaf platter, and a couple of truckers were sucking down caffeine and yukking it up with the waitress.

Everyone was either talking or thinking too loudly when Alex spotted the trio outside.

Cam thought she heard her sister saying something, but caught up in her own horror movie about the body in the trailer, and with Luce chattering nonstop opposite her, and Andy's loud slurping, she missed Alex's *Yo, it's them!*

Hello! Alex cleared her throat, coughed, and finally got Cam to look at her. *Check out the door. Look who's there.*

Cam turned. "Who?" she asked aloud.

Alex rolled her eyes, disgusted.

Lucinda turned to Cam. "Who what?" she asked.

Aw, no. Not now, Alex heard Evan grumble to himself as he spotted the trio of boys moving toward them.

All three were dressed in black. Two, who Cam guessed were the Applebees because of their resemblance to each other — small puffy eyes, wide pug noses, and humorless thin lips — were both wearing beat-up black parkas that had a greasy sheen to them from too many seasons of wear. There was something about the coats that seemed familiar.

The shorter of the two boys had a black kerchief tied around his head. *Riggs,* Alex silently identified him. The other brother's head was bare; his wet hair rubberbanded back in a scraggly ponytail. A familiar ponytail, Cam thought with a shiver. *Kyle,* she heard. Clearly, he was the leader of the pack, and mean.

The third boy — *Derek* — wore a big felt cowboy hat with a feather in the band. He was wrapped in a black coat with a short cape attached to it, a western-

style duster that reached the ankles of his grungy, wet snakeskin boots. Despite the rough-rider costume, Cam felt that he was a fraud — as surely as she knew ponytail boy was dangerous.

The dark trio brushed past the truckers, who dropped change onto the counter for their coffees and headed for the door, deep in conversation.

"Yo, kung fu man, wassup?" the ponytailed boy called to Evan. His words were casual, easygoing, but there was a threatening edge to his tone that prickled the skin on Cam's neck. She'd heard that voice before, but where?

"Kyle, dude," Ev answered, knocking fists with him unenthusiastically.

Kyle patted his grungy jacket pockets, fished out a lighter, and began mindlessly flicking it on and off.

"Hey, Riggs," Alex greeted Kyle's younger brother. He was short but massively built, and his bristly, shaved head was covered in a black do-rag. He was also wearing black leather gloves, she noticed, with the tips cut off so his red, chapped fingers and grungy nails stuck out. They were the kind of gloves weight lifters wore, but plain dumb for this weather. It tickled Alex to see Riggs Applebee trying to look so tough. She'd known him when he was a skinny, picked-on kid in fourth grade.

Back then, the Applebees were just these dirt-poor, skinny little guys whose mom had run off and left them.

Alex had felt sorry for Riggs, who was in her class, and Kyle, who was a year older. It was a terrible time for them. Their daddy didn't know how to take care of them and they'd started looking crusty and failing at school and some kids got really brutal with them, saying — right to their faces — that the reason their mama split was because they were so dumb and dirty she couldn't stand being with them.

Up until that time, it was Derek Jasper everyone had picked on. He was the smallest kid in class, even smaller than Riggs Applebee, he had a high squeaky voice, which changed by the time they started middle school, and he was new to Crow Creek, having grown up on the Northern Cheyenne reservation near Busby.

Riggs and Derek had started hanging out together. At first, Alex remembered, she'd been glad for them that they'd each found a friend, found someone to "watch their backs." And, of course, they both looked up to Kyle because he was a whole year older. Then, suddenly, it seemed, they'd changed. A lot. Derek had a growth spurt and his voice didn't just get deeper, it became an angry growl. The three of them started pumping iron. By the time everyone was at Crow Creek Regional, the Applebee boys and Derek Jasper had gotten tattoos and attitude. They didn't just freeze out the kids who'd teased them, either. They wouldn't even talk to Alex, Lucinda, or

Evan, who'd been as friendly to them as fellow outcasts could be.

That was when Evan dubbed them snakes and stooges. Unfortunately, other kids picked up on it and the name stuck.

Riggs looked her up and down now. Then he recognized her. "Alex Fielding. Yo, what are you doing around here? I heard you broke out of this place —"

"Just visiting," Alex said, but Riggs had just seen Cam and his small puffy eyes were bugging. He let out a low whistle. "Jeez, you guys could be twins."

"Duh, Riggs," Lucinda murmured. "That's 'cause they are."

"Didn't you hear?" His older brother, Kyle, snickered — and Cam noticed that he had a chipped front tooth. "They cloned weird girl. Ain't that right, Piggy?"

Lucinda reddened and lowered her head. Kyle moved the flame of his lighter near her cheek.

"Quit it, Kyle," Andy hollered from his table.

Kyle blew out the flame and stuffed the lighter back into his pocket. "Man, I wouldn't take her to a dogfight 'cause I'm afraid she'd win," the ponytailed stooge taunted. His partners giggled and snickered.

Evan started to get up, but Alex grabbed his hand.

"Call me when your IQ hits room temperature," Cam blurted out.

"Whoa." Kyle turned to her. "That sounded really cold. I bet I'd be bummed if I knew what you were talking about."

The jackass chorus chimed in again with grunts and guffaws. Then the duster-wearing Derek, the tallest of the trio, even without his ten-gallon hat, reached onto Luce's plate and started to help himself to her grilled cheese.

Andy stood up. But Evan had already grabbed Luce's fork and whacked the back of Derek's hand with it. The boy yelped.

"Yo, forget it, DJ." Riggs Applebee tugged Derek away from the table.

"Sit down, hero." Kyle pushed Andy back into his chair.

"Leave him alone, you big bozo," Luce shouted at Kyle.

He glared at her for a moment, then he grinned. "Yeah, right, 'Cinder-elephant!'"

"You know Sheriff Carson comes in here all the time," Lucinda reminded Kyle, though her gaze was aimed at Andy, who looked painfully embarrassed.

"I'm shivering in my boots" was Kyle's brilliant response.

Cam felt a shock of recognition, as if she knew him, remembered his chip-toothed snarl, his menacing posture. . . .

He was looking at her now. "Yo, Doublemint girl. Something on your mind?"

Did he know what she was thinking? Was he more than just a bully; was Kyle Applebee, like Shane, one of Thantos's messengers?

Doubtful, Alex answered Cam's unspoken question, *but he is definitely a rank dude.*

Rank? Understatement alert, Cam retorted angrily. *Don't ever diss Bree to me again! Compared to your hometown clowns, she's —*

But Alex had tuned out.

"Tell them," Luce was whispering to Evan, who was looking ill since his so-called crew had showed up. "You've got to tell them. Alex can help you. I'm sure of it."

Evan gloomily dismissed his old friend. "You're sure," he whispered back. "What, are *you* going psychic now? Alex can't do anything about this. And neither can anyone else. It's going to happen, that's all. And you'd better do what I told you."

"Let's go, Fretts," Kyle ordered Evan. "We've got . . . stuff to do —"

"What kind of stuff?" Cam asked as Evan tossed his napkin on top of his half-eaten hamburger.

Kyle gave her a hard look. He pulled out his lighter again and began flicking it on and off compulsively. "Yo,

Alex Two," he warned Cam, "keep your nose out of it, okay?"

"Watch how you talk to her, Kyle. She's a friend," Evan told him, reluctantly sliding out of the booth.

"Maybe, kung fu, but where is she going to be next week, huh?" Kyle held the flame alongside Evan's cheek. Evan pushed the older boy's hand away.

"Yeah, who's going to watch your back next week?" Derek challenged him.

"So, Riggs, how've you been?" Alex tried to reroute them. "What've you been up to? Want a fry?" She held up a greasy potato stick.

"Call that a fry?" Kyle made a face as his brother reached for it.

Derek knocked the french fry out of Riggs's hand. "Yo, don't you remember from school? She's a weirdo, dude. Who knows what she did to that thing?"

Riggs Applebee shoved Derek, sending him sprawling backward against a counter stool, his hat over his eyes.

"Anyway, I like curly fries, not those limp pieces of puke you're eating," Kyle told the twins.

"No big," Alex said, focusing on the leftovers on her plate. She could picture the straight-cut potato twisting as if she'd picked one up and wrung it out, twisting and soaring up, up, up. Then the rush started in her gut.

Go for it, she could hear Cam will. Alex looked up and saw her sister smiling, smiling and rubbing the sun charm she wore around her neck.

Alex stood abruptly, accidentally flipping her plate. Food flew. A startled shout cut off Kyle's laughter. Two french fries had spiraled from the flying dish, corkscrewing into ponytail boy's nostrils.

Riggs backed off, gasped, then clamped his hand over his mouth to keep from cracking up. From the floor, Derek pushed back his ten-gallon hat and stared up, awestruck at Kyle Applebee's potato-horned nose.

Poor guy, Cam giggled silently to Alex, *I bet those fries are cold*. She stared at them — as everyone else was doing — until the tips glowed red-hot and wisps of smoke oozed from Kyle's nostrils.

His eyes went wide as a mad cow's and his outraged bellow added to the illusion. "Moo some-ding!" he hollered.

"Do something?" Cam translated.

Evan grabbed Alex's glass of water and threw its contents in Kyle's face.

The fire hissed out. Coughing and sputtering, Kyle shook his head wildly. The fries flew free. One splatted onto Derek's black cowboy hat; the other landed on his brother's black parka.

Kyle glowered. "You think that's funny," he jeered at

Alex and Cam, who were trying not to laugh. He pulled out a knife.

Evan grabbed the older boy's arm but Kyle easily shook him off.

"Give that to me!" Andy leaped up unexpectedly.

Still holding the weapon, Kyle whirled around. The knife sliced through Andy's down jacket. "Who you giving orders to college boy?" he sneered.

"Look outside, you bonehead," Lucinda called triumphantly.

They all did and saw the revolving red light of Sheriff Carson's car pulling into the diner parking lot.

CHAPTER TEN
THE MORGUE

The stooges scattered, Evan hurrying after them, as the sheriff came into the diner, with Mrs. Bass.

Andy and Lucinda might just as well have left, too. They were standing together, oblivious to everything around them. "No, really, you scared him," Alex heard Luce say breathlessly. The glowing girl began to massage her hero's shoulder.

"Mmm," Andy murmured, "that feels great. Hey, but you're the one who called him a bonehead."

Luce shrugged modestly. "Yeah, but you tried to take the knife away."

I'm going to toss, Alex thought.

Then she saw the look on Mrs. Bass's face and felt as though she really might. Clutching her stomach, she stood up. Automatically, Cam stood with her and took her hand.

"Who was it?" Cam asked.

"The body in the trailer," Alex murmured.

"We think it's him. Ike." Sheriff Carson took off his trooper's hat. "Your dad," he added respectfully.

"Ike, her dad? As if," Lucinda cried, going over to Alex. "Oh, honey, I'm sorry. Even if he was a jerk."

The sheriff turned to Alex. "We'd like you to come down to the coroner's office, just to make sure," he said softly.

"Do I have to?" Alex asked. "Mrs. Bass knows him. Lots of other people in town do, too."

"Actually, I'd like to talk with you, anyway. I mean, I'm new here and there are things you'd know about Mr. Fielding that I don't. Like most everything." The sheriff smiled good-naturedly. "It'd be a big help if you would."

Cam watched her twin's face, concentrated hard on what Alex was thinking. *Okay. Might as well*, she heard her sister decide.

"I'm coming with you," she said softly, following Alex out of the booth.

Alex nodded. "We'll be right out," she told the sheriff and Mrs. Bass.

"What's up?" Cam asked as soon as they left.

"I feel sick."

"Well, sure," Cam said consolingly. "He was a loser, but still —"

"No. Well, yeah. But that's not all of it. Luce definitely knows something about what Evan's up to. She was trying to get him to tell me what was going on —"

Cam glanced at Lucinda and Andy. "No use trying to break into her brain. It's mush at the moment. She is so not about Evan right now." Cam smiled despite the queasiness in her stomach. "Later for that, okay?"

"Right. First things first. Ever been to a morgue before?" Nervousness made Alex giggle.

"Duh, no," Cam said sarcastically. "Don't know how I missed it. You take me to all the best places."

Fifteen minutes later, there was no sarcasm or giggling left in them.

Cam stood outside the coroner's office. "Stood" didn't exactly nail it. She was propped against the concrete wall, her head hanging down, her shoulders hunched forward. Sweat soaked her burning face as she tried with all her might to forget the grayish-white corpse. It had been lying under the plastic sheet that the doctor pulled back so that Alex could see and identify it.

Not *it*, Cam told herself. Him.

Alex had seen him all right. They both had. Only Alex hadn't thrown up. Cam had.

She'd gotten increasingly jittery waiting to go into the morgue, waiting while Sheriff Carson interviewed Alex about Ike. So by the time they'd walked into the basement room, she was primed to hurl.

At least, Cam thought, she'd made it to the sink instead of spewing on the corpse.

Alex hadn't puked, but her eyes had teared up. For a minute, Cam thought her sister was crying. But no. She had teared up because of the stinging combo of formaldehyde, antiseptic, and detergent the morgue was awash in.

The doctor had come over to the sink — after Cam had guiltily rinsed it out — and suggested that she might be more comfortable outside.

No argument. She fled. While Alex stood staring down at the body on the gleaming metal slab.

He was the color of cement. Gray. His hair. His face and neck and scrawny chest. All bloodlessly gray. All except for his arm. One arm. Which was the thing that had pushed Cam over the line.

The dead man's right arm — a patch of it, anyway — was covered in bumps, green boils, reeking like ripe cheese right through the other harsh odors in the room. The patch of putrid skin extended all the way down to

his hand, which was bent into a claw shape and had thick yellow nails.

The door to the morgue opened and Alex came out.

"Was it him?" Cam asked.

Alex nodded. "Ike," she said, and cleared her voice. "It was a double whammy, the coroner said," she went on. "He had a blowout, a doubleheader: His brain exploded and his heart gave out — from a sudden surge in blood pressure. Get this — 'brought on by stress.'" She shook her head. "Ike Fielding didn't get stressed; he *gave* it."

"Oh, wow, I'm sorry, Als."

Her sister looked at her as if she were crazy.

"I mean, I'm sorry I tossed back there. But also," Cam said with defiant honesty, "I'm sorry it was him, Ike, your stepdad. I just . . . I never saw anyone dead."

"Scared to death," Alex said. "That's what they think happened to him. I guess he was staying at the trailer and someone or something got inside and freaked him out — permanently. And that first thing I smelled? It was gasoline. They think Ike was trying to keep warm or something. There were piles of newspapers and rags soaked in gasoline." She was crying now, Cam saw.

Mrs. Bass came down the stairs. She put an arm around each of them and led them out to the parking lot, where Sheriff Carson was waiting to drive them home. Once there, the librarian offered to fix them some tea,

but Cam and Alex said they'd rather just lie down in their room for a while.

Cam pulled out her cell phone as soon as they were behind closed doors.

"I don't believe you," Alex groused. "You're going to CNN our excellent adventure? Who's the lucky callee, Beth or Bree?" Alex threw herself back on her bed.

"Brush up your mojo, Als," Cam said gently. "I've got to tell the 'rents. They're going to find out, anyway."

Cam made the call, reached Dave, and spilled the story, adding lots of assurances that they were all right and being taken care of by Mrs. Bass and Sheriff Carson.

By the time she got off the phone, Alex was sitting up again. "Guess what?" Cam said, to change the subject. "Dave heard that Bree's dad bailed on her birthday party and took off for Mexico, where some movie he's making ran into trouble or something —" Cam realized that her sister was shaking and looking extremely ill. "Als . . . are you all right?"

"All right? I just saw this corpse who I once knew, live and in color. He was . . . stone gray." Alex covered her face. "All except for that arm, which looked nothing like eczema. And his fingers were sprouting yellow claws!"

"I know. It was gross. OMG, you're going to lose it —"

"I am not!" Alex insisted, standing suddenly. "I already did! About two minutes after you did. At the morgue," she added sheepishly. "I don't think it was an accident. Ike, I mean. I don't think he just had this heart attack and brain blowout because some possum surprised him in the trailer."

"Claws. Lizard skin. Could Ike have been a warlock, too?" Cam asked.

"I thought of that. But, no, I just never got that vibe from him. Plus he was a loser. If he'd been able to cast spells, make potions, or shape-shift, he wouldn't have owed everybody something."

"I guess," Cam tentatively agreed.

"My take." Alex began to pace. "Something seriously horrible shocked or scared old Ike so bad it blew his mind, literally. Although that doesn't explain what happened to his arm. Or that nauseating odor —"

"That's why I thought it was Fredo — or Fredo's doing," Cam explained.

"But he's so lame." Alex shook her head. "Lucky for us, he's always botched things."

"He's *not* Thantos," Cam added.

Alex nodded and, a moment later, tried out a new possibility. "Thantos killed Ike — and made it look like a heart attack or whatever."

"He probably went to the trailer looking for us!" Cam gasped.

"Remember that ranch you and your family used the first time you came out here?" Alex sat again on the edge of her bed and leaned toward her sister. "And that portrait you saw of the black-bearded man — SOT NAHT — who turned out to be Thantos. It was his place, Cam. He's here. In Montana!"

"I just had this whack thought," Cam whispered, hugging herself against the cold bolt of fright slashing at her chest. "Maybe he's behind Evan's troubles, too. Maybe Thantos put Ev in danger just to lure us here."

Alex thrust her palm at her twin, signaling her to stop, to be quiet. A second later, she jumped up from the bed, crossed the room in three strides, and listened at the door. "Someone's coming."

"Mrs. Bass?"

Alex sniffed the air. "No way."

"Could you have picked a trashier town? As if the cold on Coventry Island weren't enough." Ileana was at the door, stamping her feet and shivering in her velvet cape. "Hello. Gape much?" Trailing a scent of pine needles and mint, their guardian swept into the room, slamming the door behind her.

"Ileana, what are you doing here?"

"I might ask you the same question. I thought you were safe and settled in Marble Bay. But wouldn't that be *too* convenient? As for me, I'm multitasking," the beautiful witch answered. "One of your uncles is on the loose again and as determined as ever to catch and control you. So, you know the drill, beware."

"Beware?" Cam said sourly. "Is that it? That's what you came to tell us?"

No, Alex thought suddenly. She came because of Ike. She knew something terrible had happened to him.

"Aren't you supposed to be the serene, accepting twin?" Ileana ignored Alex and raised an eyebrow at Cam. "No, that is not it. I'm here to offer you a handy hint. Apparently, Lord Thantos has forbidden his numbskull brother to play his favorite and only trick. Under threat of severe pain and punishment, Fredo is no longer permitted to shape-shift into a lizard. Without that ability, he's little more than a heartless, evil-tempered coward. Which means you won't really need me hanging around to hold your hands, will you? I mean, I do have other interests."

"Where's Mrs. Bass?" Alex asked.

"Gone biddy-bye. I expect she's arriving at the library by now. A little birdie told her she was desperately needed there."

Alex smiled. It seemed like years since she'd done it. Her face muscles felt rusty.

"But what about Thantos?" Cam began.

"Hello. Not finished," Ileana declared. With a flourish, she drew from her cape a supermarket tabloid with its usual shocker headline. This one read: MYSTERY MAN UNMASKED! And under a blurry close-up of a huge bearded brute glaring threateningly at the camera: BILLIONAIRE RECLUSE SNAPPED BY STARSTRUCK'S INTREPID CAMERAMAN.

"It's Thantos!" Alex marveled.

"Billionaire Recluse? It can't be," Cam said, though it certainly looked like their hulking uncle. With a nod from Ileana, they flipped to the article on the inside page. It was headed, CAMERA-SHY TECHNOLOGY BILLIONAIRE, SOT NAHT DUBAER, ENTERS CLINIC.

The story described their uncle as the rarely seen but powerful head of a computer empire begun in partnership with his brilliant, mysteriously murdered brother, Aron. It didn't say where the photo had been taken, or at which clinic — just that it was a rehab center for wealthy people.

"So you see, the bearded one has left the building. Lord Thantos is no longer in this tacky neighborhood. I also came to help you with your . . . other issue." Ileana peeked out the window, then stepped back so that Cam and Alex could see Lucinda climbing out of her father's car. "In response, of course, to someone's 911."

Alex glanced at Cam, who shrugged. "I didn't, like,

really ask," she protested. "I only wished Karsh were here. You were the one who called for help at the stream."

"*I* am your guardian," Ileana reminded them. "Anyway, Lord Karsh is far too . . . busy. And I haven't got a lot of time myself. You wanted help with what?"

"My friend Evan's in trouble," Alex said, "but he refuses to talk about what's going on."

"And Lucinda knows something about it but doesn't want to tell," Cam jumped in.

"For that, you summoned me?" Ileana rolled her lovely gray eyes. "Surely you can pick the girl's brain. It doesn't look that formidable —"

"It's not just Luce," Alex pointed out. She wanted to talk about Ike, to ask Ileana if she knew what had happened. But the witch's flashing eyes told her not to. "What I mean," Alex backpedaled, "is even if we can persuade Luce to tell us what she knows, there are three bad guys involved who could seriously get in the way of our trying to help Evan."

The doorbell rang downstairs. And Ileana, as if she were answering Alex's unspoken question, said pointedly, "The nice thing about having heartless, evil-tempered uncles, is that if you want somebody out of the way, you always have help."

CHAPTER ELEVEN
THE TRUTH INDUCER

As Alex and Cam let Lucinda in, Ileana sailed toward the kitchen. By the time Cam rushed after her, the edgy witch was gone. The only clues to her whereabouts were a fading scent of pine needles and mint and the squeak of the back-porch door as it swung open and shut in the wind.

"You're supposed to help us!" Cam called angrily into the stormy afternoon, then slammed the porch door. On her way back into the kitchen, she stumbled over a midnight-blue pouch lying on the floor.

Inside the velvet sack, she found a large glinting crystal, a little herb bouquet, and a tiny book of spells.

Cam sniffed at the fragrant herbs, then tasted one. It left an odd but pleasant tangy sweetness on her tongue.

A moment later, she heard herself say, "I miss Shane but Andy Yatz is such the bomb. If Lucinda wasn't desperately crushed on him, I'd so make a play for the boy."

Stunned, Cam nearly dropped the petite bouquet. Where had *that* speech come from, she wondered. Never mind that it was the truth, what had made her blurt it out? She glanced suspiciously at the herbs, then smiled slyly.

When she returned to the living room, she was carrying a cup of cocoa. "You must be freezing," she said compassionately to Lucinda. "Here, this will warm you up."

Gratefully, Luce took the cup, while Alex stared steely-eyed at her sister. *What's with the Henrietta Homemaker moment?*

"Whoops. Right back," Cam said, still wearing her gracious hostess grin. "I left something in the kitchen —"

Leafing through the miniature book, she returned to the living room, where Alex grumpily reported, *Nothing. No deal. Her head is totally clogged with Andy. It's all she can talk or think about.*

Cam dropped the velvet pouch into her sister's lap. *Compliments of Karsh's picky partner. Plus she left this*

informative little study guide. Ah, here's a nice one. It's called the Truth Inducer —"

"So, anyway," Lucinda continued, oblivious, "he's, like, so brave. I mean, I always knew he was so cute, so fine. But I never suspected how, like, you know, brave he could be. I mean, did you even see the way he stood up to those snakes? I just wanted to —"

Alex was examining Ileana's crystal. Glancing at Cam, who nodded, she tossed the glittering stone to Luce.

"Lucinda," Cam said to the startled girl. "You want us to help Evan, right?"

"How about filling us in on everything you know?" Alex pressed.

Guiltily, Luce looked down at the faceted rock in her hands. "I . . . you guys, I really can't tell you any more than I already did —"

"But not because you don't know," Alex said.

Lucinda began to mindlessly rub the crystal. "I promised him. He made me promise. I wish I could —"

At least she's telling the truth about that, Alex told her sister. *What happened to the Truth Inducer?*

You won't believe this. Cam was grinning. *It's an incantation we already know.* "How's that cocoa?" she asked Luce.

"Oh," the befuddled girl answered, "I haven't tasted it yet." She took a big sip, smiled, then began to cough.

"Lucinda." Alex leaned toward her as Cam handed the sputtering girl a napkin. "We can't help Evan without your help."

Luce's eyes were watering. She blotted her lips and cleared her throat. "That is, like, the finest hot chocolate I've ever tasted."

"Isn't it just deliciously sweet but with a spicy edge?"

Yo, Martha Stewart, get on with it! Alex silently urged her sister. *Enchant the girl.*

"No probs," Cam said brightly. "Remember this one? *Oh, sun that gives us light and cheer, shine through me now to banish fear —*"

Hold your sun charm, Alex instructed. Grasping her own hammered-gold moon amulet, she recited, *"Free Lucinda from doubt and blame. Let us win her trust —"*

"And lift her shame," Cam finished, feeling the heat of her necklace ripple through her fingertips.

"Evan told me not to go to the Crow Creek High football game this Sunday. It's a home game," Lucinda said, then took another sip of cocoa — while Cam and Alex glanced at each other, pleased that the spell seemed to be working.

"He wouldn't tell me why, but he was, like, really serious," Luce said, licking her lips. "I'm afraid something bad is going to happen. I mean, really bad."

The moment she finished, Lucinda's eyes flooded with tears.

"So something bad is going to happen at the school football game?" Alex tried to lead her gently.

"Like what?" Cam asked, sitting cross-legged on the floor in front of Luce.

"I don't know. Evan wouldn't tell me," Lucinda answered. "I mean, of course, I could be getting creeped out over nothing —"

"How bad?" Alex cut her off. "Like weapons?"

"I don't know," Lucinda cried.

Were they going to stab someone at the game? Cam wondered, horrified. Was that why there was a knife in Evan's locker? Could they be involved in Ike's death?

Cam shuddered. It wasn't Evan's crew who'd killed Ike, even if somehow they had busted into that sardine can her sister had once called home. It had to be Thantos. He had killed before. He had killed their father. He was a tracker, a powerful warlock. He could be at a clinic in Kathmandu one minute and a Montana mobile home the next.

Cam closed her eyes and tried to call up the images of her vision. Was Thantos there, lurking in the shadows? Who was the crying woman in black? Cam tried to hone in on the red container being passed to Evan by . . . Kyle. Yes, she recognized the ponytailed, chip-toothed boy

now. It was definitely Kyle Applebee. But what was in the container that Evan kept trying to push away?

A bomb? Alex suggested silently.

Now you're breaking into my visions?! Cam shot back, annoyed.

I was trying to help, Alex answered defensively. *And this is not the time to get possessive about your powers!*

"Luce." Alex put her arm around her frightened friend. "Something's going to happen first. Before school starts. Before the football game. Something at" — she looked to her sister for confirmation — "Big Sky?"

Cam nodded. "The place where Alex and I met, where you and Evan and Als worked last summer."

"Oh, you mean the tattoo thing?" Luce asked innocently.

"Tattoo?" Alex echoed.

"Um, yeah, Ev said something about getting one of those rattlesnake tattoos. But it can't be at Big Sky. The park is closed for the winter —"

"That's where it's going to happen." Cam was suddenly sure.

"Where what's going to happen?" Luce asked.

Realizing her mistake, Cam sent her sister the rest of the message silently. *That's where Kyle is going to force him to take whatever is in that container and to*

do what he doesn't want to do. We've got to get to Evan, warn him.

Alex agreed and leaped up. "Thanks, Luce. Gotta go now," she announced. Halfway to her jacket, which was hanging in the hall, she screeched to a stop. "How?!" she moaned. Turning back to Lucinda, she asked urgently, "When's your dad picking you up?"

"Um, I told him I'd get a lift home with Mrs. Bass," Luce answered, startled, coming out of her trance.

Without warning, a cheery voice — that seemed to be coming from Lucinda's hip — chimed, "You've got mail!" Luce yipped and jumped off the sofa.

"My laptop!" Cam exclaimed, fishing the compact little computer from between the couch cushions where it had slid. She opened the machine and there it was, a message from callmegoddess@coventryisland.com — also known as Ileana. Task three, successfully completed. Sit tight, the e-mail read. Your friend is on his way.

"Evan's here!" Lucinda called out.

Cam and Alex hurried after her to the door. One look at the befuddled boy told them that he didn't know any more than they did. Possibly even less, Alex decided, since she and Cam thought Thantos might be involved.

"Oh, wow, we were just talking about you." Lucinda, who hadn't read Cam's e-mail, pulled Evan inside.

Smiling glumly, he said, "Yeah, I had a feeling. I guess that's why I came. I mean, I don't know." He shrugged. "Something told me to drive over —"

"Well, have some cocoa and relax," Alex coaxed him.

"Hey, look at this." As if she were working with them, Lucinda tossed Evan the crystal.

"Cam," Alex called, "come into the kitchen with me. Let's get some hot chocolate for Ev."

"It's totally yummy," Luce told him, draining her cup, as the twins left the room.

"Will the incantation work from in here?" Alex asked.

"Worth a try."

After reciting the spell and keeping Luce from drinking most of Evan's cocoa, the boy and his brain were wide open to them. It took less than five minutes to check out their hunch that he was clueless about what was really going to happen at Big Sky.

Evan actually believed he was going to the deserted park for some bogus ceremony that included getting a rattlesnake tattoo. But when they quizzed him about why he'd told Lucinda not to show up at the football game, he broke down, big-time.

It had all gotten way out of hand, he insisted. At first they were just going to scare a teacher and some kids the Applebees had it in for. Then, slowly, he'd realized they were crazier than he'd thought. Totally ballistic. They'd started talking about torching the school — with everyone watching, everyone there for the big football game. And Evan was supposed to be the lookout.

"Why didn't you tell anyone?" Alex demanded.

"I tried!" Evan shouted back. "I wrote a note to Mr. Adamson, the coach, telling him there was trouble coming. But he took it personally, thought someone was threatening *him*, not the whole school. And he recognized my handwriting and I got suspended! I know it's lame. I could have told someone else. Done something else. But by then the knife thing had gone down and Kyle had warned me about my moms —"

"What about her?" Cam pressed.

"He said if anything went wrong, if I chickened out, they'd get my moms, hurt her bad, get her locked away in some nuthouse or arrested for neglecting the kids —"

Lucinda put her arm around Evan's shoulder.

"When is this ceremony supposed to happen?" Alex asked.

"Tonight," Evan said. Saturday night.

CHAPTER TWELVE
AN UNCLE IN EVAN'S CLOTHING

"We're going with you," Alex decided. "You go home and get ready. Pick us up on your way to Big Sky."

"Get out!" Lucinda was thrilled. "I knew you'd help!"

But Evan looked more troubled than grateful. "Forget it. The two of you against the Applebees and Derek Jasper? It won't work. You can't help me. I've got to handle this alone."

"Trust me," Alex urged him. "We're stronger than we look —"

"Whatever." Evan cut off the discussion. "I appreciate it, you guys. Honest. But I'll find a way . . . to stop them, talk them out of it —"

"Evan, you've got to believe me. We can help. Just stop by and get us tonight, okay?" Alex persisted, walking Luce and Evan to the door.

"Als, what if we can't stop the bad guys? Shouldn't we tell someone what we think is going to happen?" Cam asked when her sister returned. "Maybe not the cops yet because Evan's in the middle. But think of all the kids who knew what was going on before things went down at other schools. Big things, with guns and bombs. The kids who knew could have prevented it if they'd only told a teacher about it —"

"We'll leave a note for Mrs. Bass," Alex answered without hesitation. "She'll warn the sheriff and the school —"

But Cam had moved on to another worry. "What if Evan decides to go alone? What if he doesn't come and get us tonight?"

They could hear the pickup warming up in the driveway. "We'll go with him now," Alex said. She threw open a window and hollered for Evan to hang on a minute.

"Thanks for waiting," Cam said, climbing into the truck.

"Peuw!" Alex made a face. "Clean your wheels much? Hey, where's Luce?"

Cam couldn't control herself. "Ugh, something

stinks," she blurted, then tried to be subtle about holding her nose.

"Evan?" Alex said uncertainly.

Their driver turned toward them.

"Fredo!" they both screamed at the skinny man with the wispy whiskers, wearing Evan's knit cap and black sweatshirt.

"*Uncle* Fredo to you," he smirked.

"So it was you. I knew it!" Cam shouted.

Alex tried to open her door, but it was locked. "Let us out!" she cried, rattling the handle.

"No way are we going anywhere with you!" Cam railed, though she was feeling faint.

"Where's Evan?" Cam demanded, shaking but so angry she stopped pinching her nostrils — and immediately regretted it.

"My dear nieces," Fredo began in his high-pitched whine.

Alex pulled off her steel-toed boot and aimed it at the windshield.

"This is your friend's property. Think twice, Artemis!" He jerked his thumb toward the back of the truck. Evan and Lucinda were laid out on the flatbed, with a waterproof tarp pulled up to their chins.

"Did you kill them?" Alex asked, panicked. "Like you killed Ike?"

"Certainly not! Who's Ike? Oh, you mean your daddy?" Fredo said mockingly.

"He wasn't our father," Cam shouted. "And you know that! He's just this freak Sara married before she adopted my sister."

"Forgive me." Fredo smiled, his thin mustache stretching like a worm across his upper lip. "You girls have had so many fathers, I get confused. Well, I didn't exactly kill the Ikey one. No, that rag-wrapped package was a gift from the master."

"A gift? Yeech!" Alex was disgusted. "What master are you talking about?"

"My *gifted* brother, Thantos." Fredo looked delighted with his pun. "He wished only to save you the *inconvenience* of having Ike interfere with the guardianship hearing. He knows how fond both of you are of David Barnes, yet another adoring daddy —"

"So Thantos murdered Ike?!" Cam gasped.

"Did I say that?" Fredo put a finger to his lips. "I don't believe I mentioned murder, did I? I'm not authorized to discuss that. Just to say that he'd given you a present. Gotten Ikey out of the way. For you. A gift. You really ought to get to know him. He's very generous."

"With corpses!" Close to gagging, Alex tried not to inhale while putting on her boot. It was impossible. "So

what are you supposed to do now, turn into a giant lizard and whisk us off to Thantos-ville?"

He can't! Cam suddenly remembered.

Forbidden. Alex recalled Ileana's message. *Under threat of severe pain and punishment.*

"Would that I could," Fredo said aloud at the same time. "It's not permitted. No more. Farewell, scales and claws, fiery breath and fearsome growl," he recited wistfully. "No, I've got to bring you to him through my own resources — which my brother is always reminding me are mighty slim."

Suddenly, Fredo seemed less terrifying. He was too . . . small, thin, putrid-smelling, Alex thought. If they could wake Evan and Lucinda, the four of them could easily overwhelm him.

We could, Cam agreed. *But do we really want to? Or should we use him to help us help Evan?*

What did Ileana say? Alex asked.

"The nice thing about having heartless, evil-tempered uncles is that if you want somebody out of the way, you always have help," Cam recited.

"I would be delighted!" Fredo screeched unexpectedly. "Delighted to help you — in exchange, of course, for your cooperation!"

"No way!" Alex declared. A nanosecond later, realiz-

ing that their uncle had invaded their thoughts, she began to tremble.

Cam quickly grabbed her hand, steadying her — and said, with sugar-sweet innocence and sympathy, "A brother who's always dissing you? Gee, Uncle Fredo, what kind of brother is that?"

"It's . . . unfair," Alex chimed in, eyes wide and watering from his stench. "If you and Lord Thantos are brothers, why should he get to tell you what to do?"

"He's the smart one. Or so he thinks," their rank uncle brooded. "He said if I shape-shifted into a lizard again, I'd be finished. Of course, he didn't say I couldn't turn someone else into a raging reptile." Fredo brightened abruptly. "Especially to freak and frighten one who richly deserves it."

Her stepfather's arm — the green boils and claw-like hand. Alex felt weak. "You tried to turn Ike into a lizard," she accused.

"I am but my brother's servant." Fredo giggled nervously. "I couldn't have guessed that his prey was such a weak-hearted nervous Nellie. Truly, I'd rather have morphed myself."

"But Thantos knew. He knew Ike could be scared to death," Cam whispered, horrified. "He killed him."

"He willed it." Fredo bowed his head respectfully.

Alex shuddered, thinking of Sara's hapless husband.

How Ike must have been tortured and taunted. How terrified he must have been. Mean and selfish as Ike was, she wouldn't have wished such an awful end on anyone. But now she fixed a tender smile on her face and assured her unctuous uncle, "You'll morph again. Who wouldn't want to become big, powerful, pimply, and awesome? I've got an idea!"

"Of course," Cam echoed, as though the same thought had just occurred to her. "Uncle Fredo, Lord Thantos wants you to bring us to him. He'd be so grateful if you did —"

"Grateful? He'd totally bug," Alex exclaimed. "Ha! That would show him how wrong he was about you."

"So here's the deal," Cam said. "You help us rescue our friend Evan —"

"And we'll make sure that Thantos won't harm you," Alex interrupted, before Cam promised more than they'd deliver. "Not one little bit."

"So if I help you, you'll come back with me?" Fredo couldn't hide his excitement.

"Hmmm," Cam mused, "now what could Uncle Fredo possibly do that would frighten those snakes and stooges?"

Realizing that their uncle could tune into their thoughts, Alex tried hard not to concentrate on the answer — which was that they could convince Fredo to morph again, killing two lizards with one stone. In his mean green beast mode, their uncle could scare DJ and the Applebees *and* infuriate Thantos at the same time.

"Okay," she announced, surprised at how confident she sounded when inside she was jelly — over Ike's death, the hideous trip to the morgue, knowing that Thantos had killed again. "Wake up Lucinda and Evan, make sure they get home okay, and we'll meet you tonight at this frontier park called Big Sky."

"Really?" Fredo said warily. "You would come with me?" Fredo wriggled out of the driver's seat and walked around to the back end of the truck to revive Evan and Lucinda. "You'd tell my brother that you came because I demanded it? That *would* be sweet. I can just picture the look on Thantos's face."

"I can picture the one on Ileana's," Alex whispered.

"We're not going to summon her again, are we?" Cam asked nervously. "She said she was busy —"

"Wake up and smell Uncle Fredo," Alex cut her off. "After we get him to disobey his cranky bro by going reptile again, who's going to take him home to Coventry Island? Not me. We need all the help we can get and — when it comes to capturing Fredo — so does Ileana."

CHAPTER THIRTEEN
A PROMISE KEPT

"But I just left them!" the beautiful gray-eyed witch cried when Lord Karsh told her she'd been sent for again by the twins.

In the snow-drenched boots she hadn't had time to take off, Ileana squished back and forth on the stone floor of his cottage, angrily arguing a case she knew she'd already lost.

"I was on my way to visit Brice Stanley on the set of his new movie. I only stopped by to see how you were doing."

Lord Karsh's friend, the exalted elder Lady Rhianna, was watching her through twinkling dark eyes. Plump, brown, and dimpled, she had always reminded Ileana of a potato. It was hard to believe that the dimpled dumpling was head of Coventry Island's powerful Unity Council.

In her absence, Rhianna had been caring for the bedridden tracker — who, Ileana noted, seemed disgustingly happy to be doted on. Now, Rhianna said, "Why don't I give you two some privacy."

Yes, why don't you?! Ileana seethed silently, knowing that Rhianna would have no trouble reading her mind.

Ileana followed Rhianna to the door, slammed it shut behind her, then turned at once to Karsh. "Clearly you're much improved," she huffed. "In fact, after two sips of Lady Potato's chicken soup you should be well enough to answer the twins' SOS yourself!"

"It's not my job, Ileana," Karsh said gently. "You are their guardian. You must help them."

"And you are *my* guardian and must help *me*!" Ileana sat at the hearth and pulled off her boots. "I've put off my visit to Brice for months!" she wailed, massaging her frigid toes.

Karsh smiled affectionately at the furious, forlorn young witch. "Now as always, Ileana, your first duty is to the twins. But, of course, if I can help —"

"Fine. I'll go!" Ileana pouted. "But only under one condition — that you answer a question for me finally."

"Very well," Karsh agreed.

"I am . . ." Strangely uneasy, Ileana glanced down, away from her guardian's expectant face. "I am . . . related to them, to the twins? Aren't I? The color of our eyes . . . well, it's unusual, isn't it? It's the same color Lord Aron's eyes were. Was he my father?"

Karsh sighed. "You are of his family," he answered after a pause in which Ileana was certain he could hear her loudly beating heart. "But, no, Aron was not your father —"

"But then why —"

"I've kept my part of the bargain," Karsh insisted, cutting short her question. "Now you must keep yours. Tell the girls to meet you . . ." He hesitated thoughtfully, then seemed to come to an important decision.

Ileana waited anxiously, sure that Karsh had changed his mind, that he'd decided to tell her more about her family. Her stomach flipped in disappointment when all the old warlock said was: "A few miles outside of Crow Creek, there is a delightful glen where warm water flows. Alexandra knows the place and so, I trust, does Camryn by now. It's the place where I gave Sara the infant Artemis, fifteen years ago. That is where they should meet you."

CHAPTER FOURTEEN
ANCESTRAL VOICES

"I don't suppose our guardian goddess mentioned how we're supposed to get there," Alex grumbled, buttoning her jacket and reaching for the woolen scarf hanging on the coatrack in Mrs. Bass's hallway.

"Sara's stream in fifteen minutes." Cam shut her laptop. "That's all she wrote. Nothing about transportation."

As her sister bundled into her hot-pink ski parka, Alex stared gloomily out the window. There was no way they could get to the stream that fast.

It was almost four o'clock. They were supposed to meet Evan at Big Sky at five-thirty — Evan and Uncle Stinko. The winter sun had already set. Only a full moon shining on sparkling snow lit the world outside.

"Transportation, transportation," Alex mused.

"Did you write the note to Mrs. Bass?" her sister asked.

"Mm," Alex said, distracted.

"The note about what's going to happen tomorrow?" Cam persisted.

"Of course." Alex turned suddenly from the window. "Cam, the spell book, didn't it have —?"

"The Transporter." Cam understood at once.

They scrambled to find the velvet purse and the little book Ileana had left for them. Cam turned quickly to the page. "Here it is: the Transporter!"

In addition to reciting the incantation, what they needed, the book said, was fire for enthusiasm, passion, and desire —"

"We can light candles," Cam decided, racing for the four candleholders on the dining room table. "And mugwort," she read, returning, "the traveler's herb."

"Mugwort?" Alex ran into the kitchen and checked the spice shelf. No mugwort. The closest thing to it was marjoram. It would have to do. "Okay, what else?" she asked, sprinting back to Cam with the herb.

"A magick circle. We're supposed to sit inside it, facing east. What are you doing?" Cam asked, aghast, as her sister opened the spice jar and sprinkled a sloppy circle of marjoram flakes onto the clean floor.

Pulling the knit cap from her jacket pocket, Alex drew it over her spiky platinum hair, then stepped into the circle and sat down. "East? That would be —" Carefully, she adjusted her direction. "Okay, what else?"

"Just the incantation. I'll read it over once, all right?" Cam said. "Then we'll do the whole thing together."

"We haven't got a lot of time," Alex decided. "Light the candles."

Cam did, placing them on the floor near her sister and, as Alex set the candles at the four sides of the circle, Cam read the spell — which ended in: *"Good magick like air and water flow, transport me body and spirit now."*

A sudden breeze tickled Cam's neck and set the candle flames flickering. She looked around for the open window. When she turned back, Alex was gone!

"Cam?" In her arctic gear, Alex stood in the warm fog beside the stream. Blinded by beads of sweat flowing like a waterfall from under her woolen hat, she called out again, "Cam? Where are you?"

A minute later — auburn hair standing on end like electrified dandelion froth, eyes, ears, and nose wind-burned and raw — her sister landed. "It worked!" Cam exclaimed. "Is she here yet?"

With the roar of a tornado, the fog before them

swirled and twisted. "Who are you? Who dares disturb my peace?" a voice boomed from the spiraling mist.

The voice was not Ileana's. It was deeper, more commanding, yet breathless, wheezing with age.

The twins peered at the churning vapor and together saw the hazy form of a woman take shape. Though she was holding a cane, her back was ramrod straight. Eyes closed, she stood tall and resolute and utterly without gentleness, like a blind warrior, wounded but not bowed in battle.

"Um, sorry," Alex croaked, tearing off her hat, trying to blink away the salty, stinging perspiration. "I'm Alex, er, Alexandra, and this is my sister, Camryn —"

"And we didn't mean to disturb anyone," Cam said, taking Alex's hand. "Uh, do you think you could tell us —"

"Like who *you* are?" Alex asked.

"I am Leila," the ancient spirit replied. "Do you not know me?"

Alex gulped. "Well, um, Leila, I can't see you all that clearly. Cam's the one with the —"

"Impudent fledgling," the old woman hissed. And at that, her eyes flew open. "Brazen as my boys!"

Cam gasped. Leila was not blind. Her eyes were wide and piercing and gray — metallic gray, outlined in black. Her eyes were identical to Cam's and Alex's and

Ileana's. Staring at the imperious shape in the mist, Cam began to make out its other features: iron-gray hair, a strong, still-beautiful face etched with deep creases of age. And under brooding, dark eyebrows, those stunning eyes, chilling and familiar.

"Your boys?" Alex asked.

"Aron was my favorite," the woman warrior said, "my bright angel."

"Aron? You knew him?" Cam's eyes burned again, from the strain of squinting through the fog, she guessed. Or was she crying?

"He was my son!" the voice boomed again, then broke pronouncing the name. "Aron . . . I loved him best. Thantos, my eldest, was too much like me — ambitious, unyielding, and vengeful. Fredo — ah, where did he come from, my poor Fredo? My youngest and last child. Perhaps I was too old. He was never right, never as bright as the others."

Alex wondered if Cam was seeing this, hearing every word of it, but she couldn't tear her eyes from the apparition.

"Where are my grandchildren?" the spirit cried out. "Where are Aron's girls? Fredo had two sons, dullards and demons like himself —"

"But we're Aron's daughters," Alex said, glad to feel Cam's hand squeezing her own reassuringly.

"The women of our family." Ignoring or not hearing them, Leila continued. "They are the true heirs of the noble DuBaer dynasty. My granddaughters, beautiful and wise beyond their years — Artemis. Apolla. Proud Ileana . . ."

Cam glanced at Alex. *Ileana?!* Alex nodded, stunned. *That's what she said.*

"And Miranda, my beloved daughter-in-law, once the most brilliant and powerful of them all . . ."

"Miranda? She's our mother!" Cam cried out.

"Did you know her?" Alex asked. "Is she . . ."

"Alive?" Cam exclaimed hopefully.

The ancient woman seemed to see them for the first time. Her strong features softened. Her gray eyes lost their metallic glint. "Apolla, Artemis," she said, acknowledging them at last, "my dear ones." She sighed then, exhaling an apple-crisp scent of autumn leaves and the fragrant loam of earth.

"What happened to our mother? Why did she leave us?" Alex asked, even as Leila's warm breath caressed her, ruffling her spiky hair, making her eyelids irresistibly heavy.

"Does Ileana know where she is?" Cam, too, fell under the spell of the ghost warrior's soothing sigh.

"Is she . . . is Ileana our sister?" Alex asked.

Lulled by the balmy breath stroking their cheeks, they closed their eyes and, what seemed only a moment later, whirled to the sound of laughter and a mocking voice saying, "Your sister? You wish!"

Sweeping ice-draped branches out of her way, Ileana crunched toward them through the snow. Her velvet blue cape billowed behind her, its hood framing her petulant face. Draped about her neck was an odd scarf, a choker of bright, ginger-orange fur.

"Leila!" Cam shouted, turning back toward the swirling fog. "She's here. Ileana is here."

"She's gone," Alex said, releasing her sister's hand. The churning mist, from which the figure of the fierce old woman had appeared, had given way to steam rising from the flowing water and green moss along the bank.

"Where is your friend?" Ileana asked as her fur scarf unwound and began to meow.

"It's Boris!" Cam recognized Ileana's pet, the marmalade cat who scared Fredo silly.

"Who were you talking to?" Ileana looked around. "Who drove you here?"

Alex tried to stop staring at Ileana's gray eyes, mirror images of Cam's and her own, identical to Leila's. "No one drove us here," she blurted, distracted. "We were talking to our —"

"And hers," Cam reminded her sister.

"What do you mean, no one drove you here?" Ileana's glorious gray eyes glinted impatiently at the girls. "You couldn't have gotten here on your own. And I distinctly heard you yammering to someone other than your saucy selves."

"Ileana, we saw something, someone. A tall, tough old lady —" Alex tried again.

Ileana waved her arm and snapped her fingers. "Enough!" she announced. "I get it now!" The cat purred loudly, nuzzling her white neck. Ileana stroked the creature mindlessly. "You misused the book I lent you! You performed an unauthorized spell, didn't you? And where, I'd like to know, did you find mugwort in this forsaken meat-freezer of a town?"

"Um, we didn't know we weren't allowed to use the spells," Cam confessed. "And we used marjoram."

"Marjoram! Clever T*Witches. And just how did you know that marjoram was a travel herb?"

They looked at each other, surprised.

"In ancient times," Ileana impatiently informed them, "it was thought to be the herb that helped the dead travel to other worlds."

Our grandmother, Alex mused, and heard her sister thinking the same thing. *That's how Leila found us!*

Do you know what this means? Alex asked, trembling with excitement.

That we can learn more about our family! Cam responded, awestruck.

"Never mind. Never mind!" Too out of sorts to crash their thoughts, Ileana began to pace angrily. "Not only did you perform an unauthorized spell, but you've summoned me here wantonly —"

"You don't understand. Ileana, the most astounding thing just happened," Cam began.

Alex held up her palm. "Yo, chill, first things first," she urged, then turned to their irate guardian. "I just thought you'd want to know that an old pal of yours is going to join us tonight —"

"Fredo," Cam jumped right in. "He's meeting us at Big Sky."

"Fredo?" Ileana said.

Ileana's brain calculated so swiftly that Alex had trouble following it. All she could make out was a hodgepodge of thoughts and questions about herself and Cam, and their father, and Fredo and Thantos, and even their lost mother, Miranda —

Glancing at Cam for help, Alex saw that her sister was "otherwise engaged," all up in her head, zoning on the same cast of characters Ileana was thinking about — with Leila thrown into the mix. Before she could snap Cam out of it, Alex's attention was caught again by Ileana and the words *Mexico* and *Brice*, followed by a deep, sad sigh.

"What do you mean Fredo's going to join you?" Ileana snapped out of her reverie. "Where is the foul idiot?"

"He's supposed to meet us at Big Sky," Cam told her again, reentering Earth's orbit as if she'd never been gone. "You know, that funky theme park where Alex and I met."

Okay, if everyone was back on the planet, she'd put in her two cents, Alex decided. "He should be there any minute," she said. "And we've got to be there, too, or something very bad is going to happen —"

"And not just to Evan," Cam explained, "but to an entire school full of unsuspecting kids."

"You're certain that Fredo's going to be there?" Ileana asked, as if she hoped they were lying. Alex nodded, and the troubled witch sighed again. "Oh, all right. Come over here." She opened her cape, revealing its blindingly gold lining. "Tuck in," she ordered. "One of you on each side of me, gently holding my waist. Excuse me!" she yelped, when Alex took hold of her too hurriedly. "Gently!! As in softly, lightly. Not grab-ly. As in grip, snatch, mutilate! Subtle difference, I know, since they both begin with g —"

"Ileana, we're going to be late," Cam broke in. "Please . . ."

"Close your eyes and think of mugwort . . . leafy, sil-

ver, fragrant. Then give me your energy. Let go of it all, your will, your wants, your needs. Let go of them and hang on to me. Gently!"

As if he knew what to expect, Boris scrambled desperately into a pocket of his mistress's cloak. Alex could hear his little heart racing as he mewed pitifully; Cam felt him shivering, even as Ileana's warm cape closed around them, blocking out moonlight and snow.

Again they experienced the terrifying tornadolike roar. It was muffled this time by the thick cocoon of the velvet cloak. A second later or an hour — it was impossible to tell — the howling wind let up. The sudden silence made their ears pop.

They let go of Ileana — and landed, with a bone-wrenching thump, on the ice-coated, split-rail fence used to herd visitors toward the run-down Ferris wheel.

"Hello. Did I say, 'Unfasten your seat belts, you may move around the cabin now'?" Ileana asked, laughing wickedly.

Boris leaped from her pocket. With a tiny plunk, he disappeared into a snowbank. "Foolish feline," their guardian scolded, shaking her head at the cat-shaped hole in the snow. "Of course, he may be on the trail of your moronic uncle," she mused, kneeling to examine Boris's burrow.

He may be your moronic uncle, too, Alex wanted

to say — or your father! Instead, she and Cam climbed down from the fence, rubbing their bruised backsides.

And then an awesome thought occurred to Alex: This is how Karsh must have carried me to Marble Bay! She'd always been mystified by how she'd gotten from her Montana trailer to Cam's Massachusetts doorstep in what had seemed like the blink of an eye.

Now, not only did she know *that,* but she and Cam had just learned how to transport themselves! Again the possibilities thrilled her.

Hello! Business to take care of! Her sister called her back from her musings. The park looked exactly as Cam had dreamed it. Dark, ominous shapes loomed. Overhead, clouds flew past the full moon, leaving fast, shifting shadows below. The twins squinted into the darkness, hoping to find Evan.

Alex picked up murmured conversation. Cam saw a thin light.

"I've made my decision," Ileana announced, distracting them. "Boris and I will look for Fredo . . . for a bit. If we don't find him, I'm off to my next appointment. Fair enough?"

"He'll be here. We weren't lying," Cam whispered indignantly.

"Did I accuse you?" Ileana was equally indignant. "I was called here to help you. I did. You want me to return

the stinky cheese man to Coventry. I will. But I've got things to do, people to see —"

"Oh, right, like Brice Stanley?" Alex ragged. She immediately regretted it. Ileana furiously stared at her, and Alex was overcome with fear and nausea. Bolts of electricity careened through her body like a lead bead in a pinball machine. And, all at once, she knew that she was being transformed . . . into a woodland creature . . . something small and desperate that scrabbled through the darkness to snatch its food from under rocks.

No! she heard herself beg from a distance. And then she was well again. Breathing hard, but unharmed, unchanged.

Ileana wore a smile of dangerous satisfaction. *"Adios, amigas,"* she sang out. With a flutter of her fingertips and a wink to Alex, she left them to follow the tunneled trail Boris was making as he moved beneath the snow.

A moment later, their devious guardian had disappeared. Their attack uncle was nowhere in sight. They were alone. Camryn and Alex stared out at the swift-moving darkness.

The faint light Cam had seen moments ago was coming from a small cabin in the shadow of the Ole Wagon Wheel. It was some sort of old storage shed with two small windows. Inside, lit by the glow of oil lamps, Riggs and Derek were ransacking the place. Cam recog-

nized them by their height and head gear — Riggs, a stumpy shadow in a black bandanna; Derek, a Stetson-crowned string bean.

The voices Alex had picked up came from outside the cabin. Blowing on his hands, shifting from foot to foot in the snow, Evan was only a few feet from the log cabin's door, talking with Kyle Applebee.

"Yo, man, don't even go there," Alex heard the older boy say, his forefinger thumping Evan's shoulder for emphasis. "No way are you wimping out on us now —"

"Dude, I never said I was with you on this one," Evan argued. "I said I wouldn't rat you out. And I didn't. But get real, Kyle. You're not actually going to do this, are you? Set fire to the school —"

"No, man." Kyle's brother stepped out of the cabin. "You got it all wrong." Riggs, short, squat, and hard as a fireplug, told Evan, "He's not going to do that. You are."

CHAPTER FIFTEEN
THE AVALANCHE

"You're crazy," Evan protested.

"No, he's telling the truth." Kyle laughed. "*You're* crazy — same as your mama. Don't forget, dude, she's the one who's gonna pay if you bail on us now —"

"But he won't." Riggs clapped Evan's back. "Right, bro?"

"Don't you get it?" Evan was trying to get through to them. "You can't do it. Someone could get hurt, really hurt. Dude, I've got friends there and you guys do, too. There are lots of kids who look up to you —"

"Well, they better stay in the bleachers and out of the building." The ponytailed Kyle grinned. "Anyway, bro, we're not up to that part yet. First thing we gotta do is get you tattooed. That's why we're here."

"Yeah, that, and just one other little thing." Riggs rubbed his hands together. He was wearing his weight-lifting gloves, and the tips of his fingers were bright red with cold.

"Later," Kyle snapped at his brother. "We're not talking about that now. You ready in there?"

"We got a problem," Riggs admitted sheepishly. "No electricity. So Derek's gonna do it jailhouse style. He'll draw the snake with his fishing knife — it's not too rusty. Then we'll rub ink into the cut. Won't be as pretty as ours, but it'll work."

Evan looked around anxiously, as if trying to see out into the darkness.

"He's looking for us," Cam whispered. "I wonder where Luce is. Evan must have come alone. Alex, we have to do something."

"Like what?" Alex rasped back, the smell of pine needles suddenly sharp in her nose. In an instant, she tracked the scent to a tall fir tree overhanging the cabin. Its broad branches glistened with packed snow.

How choice would it be if a sudden wind ruffled the heavy pine needles, loosening the snow and sharp icicles, sending them crashing down onto Kyle's grungy

ponytail, down the back of his scrawny neck, walloping his rigid shoulders . . .

"Bull's-eye!" Cam whispered admiringly. "You got him!"

The avalanche Alex wished for had toppled Kyle Applebee. "Help me up!" he commanded, writhing on the ground, reaching out to his brother. But a late-falling chunk of ice broke Riggs's grip and sent him tumbling on top of Kyle.

For a moment, in disbelief, Evan watched the boys squirming and sliding in the snow. Then his good nature took over and, with Derek, who'd run outside, knife in hand, he tried to haul the brothers to their feet.

"What happened?" Derek wanted to know.

"Shut that door!" Kyle hollered viciously.

Derek ran back and pulled the metal door shut.

"Show him?" Cam said.

"I'm tired." Alex grinned. "You take the encore."

Cam did. Her gaze fueled by anger, she heated the heavy snow on the storage cabin's slanted roof, sending it sliding. A river of slush roared down on Derek's beloved ten-gallon hat, crushing his favorite feather and weighing down the hat's brim till it framed the startled boy's face like a pioneer woman's sunbonnet.

"My knife," Derek wailed, dropping to his knees in

the snow. "It fell out of my hand. It's my old man's. He doesn't even know I took it."

"You and that dumb knife. Forget it," Kyle sneered. With Evan's help, he and Riggs were on their feet again.

"You don't understand. My old man'll kill me," Derek wailed, plunging his fingers under the snow, still searching for the knife.

Did you see where it went? Alex silently asked Cam.

Of course, her supersighted twin responded. *He's inches from the blade. Whoops! He found it.*

Derek let out a hair-raising shriek. "I'm cut. I'm bleeding!"

"Get over yourself, DJ," Kyle said contemptuously. "We got more important things to do tonight than listen to you bellyache over a scratch."

"Yeah, the best is yet to come," Riggs snickered. "Come on, Kyle. Can't we do it now?"

"I'm . . . ready," Evan said, talking about the tattoo.

"Hear that?" Riggs told his brother. "He's ready."

"There's not gonna be any tattoo," Kyle told Evan. "Riggs and DJ were messing with you —"

"Yeah, like you really earned your rattlesnake. Not!" Derek sneered, wiping the blood off his cut hand with snow.

"I don't get it," Evan said. "Then what are we doing here?"

Derek and Riggs looked at each other, trying not to crack up. Then they turned to Kyle. "Yo, Ev. Let me ask you again," the older boy said. "You in with us or you out?"

"Dude, I can't do it —"

"Sure. Sure, kung fu. I understand." Kyle took Evan's arm. "Come on, got something I want to show you."

"Oh, wow. Oh, man." Riggs was ecstatic. "DJ, wait out here," he ordered, following Evan and his brother back to the cabin.

"Where's the red container?" Cam whispered. "And the woman? Everything's pretty much the way I pictured it, except for that — oh, and also that there are three guys with Evan instead of two."

"Never mind all that — where's Fredo?" Alex sniffed the blustery air. It was cold, biting, scented with pine needles and wet wood. "Great. What if Uncle Carbuncle doesn't show?" she said too loudly.

Derek looked up, nervously studying the shadows. "Who's out there?" he called softly, tentatively.

An ill-timed gust of wind shifted their cloud cover.

"Busted," Alex said, stepping from behind a tree out into the bright moonlight.

Derek's eyes widened in fear and wonder. "Alex Fielding? What are you doing here?"

Cam followed Alex into the light. "We could ask you the same question."

"Hey," Derek said, bewildered, "what's going on here? Who else is back there?" He looked past Cam as if expecting a parade of clones to march from the shadows. When it didn't, he grumbled, "My dad does security here. Me and my crew are taking his shift for tonight. Now get out."

"Don't you wish this place was open?" Alex asked, eyeing the dark disk of Ferris wheel against the cloud-dappled sky. "So you could go on a ride?"

"Ha-ha, so funny I forgot to laugh," Derek said. "I told you to beat it. Now, scat!" he ordered.

"A ride on the Ole Wagon Wheel. Excellent idea," Cam chimed in enthusiastically. *Think we can do it?*

Full moon. Necklace power. Got Ileana's crystal in my pocket. Right here with . . . Alex pulled out a crumpled piece of paper. "Uh-oh," she groaned.

"Uh-oh, what?" Cam wanted to know.

Nothing —

Cam snatched the paper from her sister's hand. *It's the note you were going to leave for Mrs. Bass!*

— *much*, Alex concluded weakly.

So if we don't succeed, tonight we'll have to let the cops know what's going to go down. And Evan will be right in the middle of it.

Hello. We are going to succeed! Pausing to consider their situation, Alex added, *We have to.*

CHAPTER SIXTEEN
LOSING DEREK

"I told you to get lost," Derek said. "Want me to spell it out for you?"

"If I remember right," Alex said, "that would be harder for you to do than for us to make you fly."

She clenched the crystal and felt bits of marjoram clinging to it. "Think of mugwort —" she called softly to Derek, who gaped at her, dumbfounded.

Rubbing the hammered-gold sun medallion their father had made for her, Cam said, "It's this really nice plant — think silver-gray, leafy . . ."

Stare at him, Alex urged, *while I come up with an incantation. Cool*, she said, a moment later. *How's this:*

"Spirits of fairness, justice, and right. Save Crow Creek High from its terrible plight —"

"You enchant, girl!" Cam cheered, her intense eyes pinning Derek.

"Help us . . ." Alex floundered. *"Er, help —"*

"Help us to do what you would want done," Cam quickly ad-libbed, *"with the magic of moonlight and the power of sun."*

Derek was staring at them. His mouth was slack and his eyes scrunched, as if he were trying to understand a tricky homework assignment. Then, suddenly, his body arched backward, arms raised, legs stretching up from his ratty snakeskin boots.

"Eyes on the prize," Alex said, calculating the distance from Derek to the Ole Wagon Wheel, which loomed behind the storage shed. "That one," she decided, focusing on one of the run-down ride's highest and most rickety carts.

Alex rubbed her half-moon charm, feeling at once the hum of energy flow in her.

"Let's blow him away," Cam said, reminded suddenly of Leila's enchanted sigh.

The same thought came to Alex. *Grandmother, help us now*, she urged. *Great spirit of the stream, Leila . . .*

They each took a deep, crystal-cold breath and, as one, expelled a blast of icy air. Derek flew! He tumbled backward like a celestial gymnast, a dark, spinning shadow in the sky. Then he landed — headfirst, on his soaked, misshapen hat — in the wobbly cart at the top of the Ole Wagon Wheel.

"Score!" Cam shouted, high-fiving her twin.

The door to the cabin opened, spilling lamplight onto the snow. "Well, well." Kyle Applebee grinned grimly. He was carrying a red container. "Who let the Twisted Sisters out?"

"The Karate Kid's got company," Riggs called, following his brother outside.

"Where's Evan?" Alex asked. But Cam was already on the case, staring at the log cabin, trying to penetrate its walls with her uncanny gray eyes.

Kyle was glaring at them. "How'd you get in here? Where's Derek?" he snarled, looking around for his crony.

"He's up —" Alex said, smiling defiantly.

"— to no good," Cam quickly cut in. A second later, she gasped. Evan was inside the cabin. A woman clothed in black was slumped against him. It was Mrs. Fretts. Wrapped in Kyle's greasy parka, Evan's mother was crying softly on her son's shoulder.

"They have his mom," Cam reported.

Spilling gasoline from the red plastic container he held, Kyle whipped around and glared at his brother. "I told you to keep that door shut!"

"You were out at the trailer, weren't you?" Alex demanded, remembering the gasoline smell.

"Wouldn't be no trailer left," Riggs snarled, "if someone hadn't dumped your old man out there. We were going to use the place for practice. Burn that dive down."

"But not with some stinking stiff inside. We woulda got nailed for murder," Kyle added. "Who's gonna believe we had nothing to do with it?"

There was a sudden commotion in the shed. Mrs. Fretts dove outside, shaking her fist at the Applebees. Evan grabbed her before she fell. Gently, he led her back toward the cabin but she refused to go inside. She leaned against the wall, arms stubbornly crossed, her distressed face trying to find a threatening expression.

"You know what?" Kyle addressed the twins, pretending to be laid-back about finding trespassers on his turf and one of his crew missing. "You want to stick around and watch? Cool. But you only get to see the previews. You won't be around for the show."

"Is that a threat?" Alex challenged.

Riggs reached inside his jacket and pulled out a gun. "That answer your question, Alex?"

"Guess so," she told the grinning boy in the black head scarf.

Okay, she could probably make the gasoline can fly out of Kyle's hand, Alex thought. Although his grip on it was pretty tight. And Cam might be able to bend the barrel of Riggs's gun, which was no cheap toy. But they could seriously use a hand right about now.

Or, even better, a claw.

Didn't happen to see Fredo in that vision, did you? Alex silently asked her sister.

I think we're on our own, Cam said.

"Let them go." It was Evan. "They don't know anything. What are they going to do, report you for attempted tattooing?"

"Too late, kung fool," Kyle said.

"It's going down tomorrow," Riggs reminded Evan. "We don't need any heat between then and now —"

"Riggs, don't you get it? If you hurt them," Evan tried to explain, "you'll have a lot more heat."

"Really?" Kyle said. "How do you figure? I mean a couple of tourist girls disappear in the woods. Happens all the time. Too bad the sheriff's office will be so busy trying to find them there'll be nobody left to patrol the football field."

OMG, Cam thought suddenly, *this is it. This is when*

it happens. She recognized not just the place, but the time, the moment.

The woman in black was Evan's mom, looking chunky in Kyle's parka.

Derek was no longer in the picture; there were only the two boys that she'd seen.

The full moon, which had played peekaboo with the clouds all night, was now totally visible and very bright —

And Kyle was holding the red container.

Smiling his broken-toothed grin, he pushed the gasoline can at Evan. "Just take it," he said. "You got to. It's too late now."

As he'd done in Cam's vision, Evan pushed it away. "No. No way, man. No."

"Okay, listen up," Kyle said. "I'm through playing. Here's the way it is. I'm not torching the school. Riggs ain't doing it. And neither is that Chicken Little, DJ —"

"You the man." Riggs laughed at Evan.

"That's right," his brother backed him. "You're going to do this thing. So take it." Again he shoved the red can at Evan. "Yo, Crouching Tiger, it's one of them deposit things. You bring the gas can back empty tomorrow, we return your moms."

"Take it!" Riggs shouted, pointing his gun at Evan's

head. "Let's go, bro. Time to move on to the bonus round. And, man, what a bonus we got ourselves. You gotta set the gas *and* barbecue old Crow Creek High, or we get to keep your mama *and* the Troublemint twins."

"Uh-oh," Cam murmured. "Lucinda wasn't kidding —"

Kyle turned to glare at her. As he did, Evan made his move. Arm stiffly bent, one leg cocked, he shouted, spun, and kicked out. The martial arts move, meant to knock the gun out of Riggs's hand, totally missed, but Evan's fierce karate cry at least startled the hefty boy into nearly dropping his weapon.

"Lucinda wasn't kidding?" Alex asked.

I had this premonition flash a second before Evan acted up, Cam explained. *Lucinda wasn't kidding. He really does bite at karate.*

Alex felt her anger rise, fueled by her love for Evan. Before Riggs had steadied himself, before Kyle took in what had gone down, she whispered to Cam, "Grab your necklace. Let's send the boy some juice!"

Cam rubbed her sun charm. Alex held tightly to her moon amulet. They felt the electric jolt rush through them and — focusing on Evan's shoddy boots — they passed their parents' powerful energy to the desperate boy.

Evan's foot lashed out again. And connected. With

Riggs's jaw. The boy fell backward. The gun flew out of his hands. It landed several feet away in the deep snow.

There was no time to gloat. Kyle tossed the gasoline can to Evan. Automatically, instinctively, Evan caught it. The flammable liquid splashed all over his clothes and face, temporarily blinding him.

Kyle backed away, laughing. "Practice makes perfect," he shouted, hunting for something in his sweatshirt pockets.

"He's looking for his lighter," Alex cried.

"He won't find it," Cam assured her. *It's in his parka — which Evan's mom is wearing.*

But Kyle remembered. He turned toward Mrs. Fretts, who began shrieking in terror.

Riggs stirred. Lifting his head from the ground, he massaged his jaw and tested his nose. "Oh, man," he murmured, shifting his nostrils. "What is that?" He inhaled once, then fell back into the snow.

Alex caught a whiff of the odor at the same time.

"Get off me, get off me!" Evan's mother tried to swat Kyle Applebee away.

"Leave her alone," Cam ordered, rashly aiming her fiery eyes at the bully.

Kyle shoved Mrs. Fretts hard against the shed and tried to search the pockets of the jacket she was wearing.

Evan's mom cried out.

Cam felt the vengeful heat gathering in her eyes. A single blink would send a bolt of flame at Kyle's scraggly ponytail.

"Wait! No!" Alex warned her, as Evan, his hooded sweatshirt soaked with gasoline, ran blindly toward his mother's screams.

Cam quickly lowered her gaze from Kyle's ponytail to the snow at his feet. But suddenly a putrid odor assailed her. "Whoops!" she gasped as Kyle's snakeskin boots burst into flames.

Alex tackled Evan, to keep him away from the fire. "Get out of that sweatshirt," she urged. Eyes stinging and shut, Evan rolled in the snow, wrestling off his sweatshirt as Kyle, trying to stomp out the boot blaze, danced wildly closer to them.

All at once he stopped. He wrinkled his nose. And gasped.

Evan hurled his gas-soaked sweatshirt. It landed on top of the red can.

There was an unearthly roar. The ground rumbled beneath them. And Alex, lying facedown in the snow, recognized the ripe swamp stench of Uncle Fredo, who, she peeked and saw, had recklessly morphed into his favorite but forbidden form.

Better late than never! Cam grumbled, seeing — and smelling — the monstrous lizard.

Freed from his feeble body, practically giddy with glee, Fredo lifted Kyle Applebee off the ground. The ponytailed bully yelped once, then promptly passed out, his boots still aflame.

Fredo grinned madly. Mrs. Fretts slid to the ground, covering her face and howling.

"Put out the fire. Blow out his boots," Cam called as her uncle lurched closer to the gasoline can hidden by Evan's sweatshirt.

Cam, Alex, and Evan flattened themselves against the ground as the repulsive reptile batted at Kyle's burning boots. They only dared look up when they heard the hiss of crackling snakeskin fizzling out in the frigid snow.

CHAPTER SEVENTEEN
FAMILY MATTERS

"Did you see that? Was I born to be huge, or what?" Fredo crowed, tossing Kyle aside.

"Why don't you slip into something more comfortable," Alex suggested, "like yourself."

"Just in case one of Thantos's spies is around," Cam reminded their uncle, holding her nose as politely as possible. "That lizard look is off-limits, remember?"

"Oh, all right." Fredo sulked. "But my brother will forgive me everything, once I bring you to him." Slowly, with obvious regret, he began returning to his human form. Which was no great improvement, Cam noted, on his revolting reptile appearance.

She was glad that Evan and his mother hadn't seen

the changing. They were both inside the cabin. Mrs. Fretts had passed out cold, with her head on Evan's lap. Evan, exhausted and still groggy from the gas fumes, leaned against a wall, resting his eyes.

"I love being a lizard," the twins' shrinking uncle confided. "And I'm good at it, aren't I? Colossal!" With a semimorphed claw, he swept back his thinning, greasy dark hair. "So, are we all set?"

"Almost," Alex said. "No hurry, right?"

"Yeah," Cam agreed. "Why don't we chill and chat, you know, about the family?"

"Which family?" Fredo asked coyly, brushing leftover lizard skin from his Coventry cape. "Yours, hers, ours? There are so many."

"Ours," Alex said. "Which, rumor has it, includes a certain beautiful guardian witch —"

Fredo's squinty eyes grew large. The smile left his face at last. "I don't know what you're talking about," he said nervously. "I never said a word about it!"

"We're talking about Ileana, of course," Cam persisted. "Whose child is she? Is she our sister? Was our father married to someone else, before he met our mother?"

"Or is Ileana Miranda's daughter by a previous marriage?" Alex asked.

"No," Fredo said.

The word, rumbling with an echo that sounded most un-Fredo-like — aggressive, angry, impatient — was followed by the sudden meowing of a cat.

The twins looked down and there was Boris. Wet, scruffy, shaking with cold, he glared at Fredo. They looked up again, and there was Ileana, in not much better shape than her pet. It was her decisive "no" that had reverberated with Fredo's.

"What is this?" Fredo demanded, backing away from Boris. "Who invited the party poopers? Did you forget that I'm allergic to cats — particularly to that one?"

Boris hissed and hunched his back. Fredo began frantically scratching his scrawny arm. "Go on, go on, try to best me as you did last time we met," he taunted Ileana. "This time, you will not have the twins' magick on your side. They are going with me — voluntarily!"

"Um, Fredo —" Cam began.

Their goat-bearded uncle could not be silenced. "All your power, both inherited and learned, may be strong enough to hurt me, Ileana, but you'll never overcome our combined strength. I am just one against you, but with the daughters of Aron and Miranda on my side, there's nothing you can do."

Ileana shook her head in disgust and turned her back on their skinny uncle. "Do you know how far away

Mexico is?" their guardian growled at Cam and Alex. "And how warm?"

"Is that where you went?" Alex asked.

Cam snapped her fingers. "You went to visit Brice, right? He's supposed to be starring in the movie that a friend of mine's father is producing —"

"Not Eric Waxman?" Ileana wrinkled her nose.

"Waxman, that's it," Cam affirmed. "He's my friend Brianna's father —"

"Father?" Alex sneered. "He's as good a father as Thantos is an uncle."

Ileana sighed. "We were having such a marvelous time until he showed up, unannounced, uninvited, and unwanted!"

"May I have your attention, please?" Fredo demanded, frantically scratching his ankle.

"Not now," Ileana grumbled, waving him away. "Just stand still and be quiet and I'll tell Boris not to rub against you."

"Yes, goddess." Fredo bowed slightly, then straightened and stood still as a statue.

"Ileana." Cam had an idea. Alex instantly seconded it. "We've got a favor to ask. . . ."

Ileana tapped her pale chin thoughtfully as they outlined their plan. Basically, it called for Ileana to spook

Eric Waxman and send him sprinting from Mexico to Marble Bay full of gratitude and dad-itude. To make good on the promise he'd made to Brianna, his daughter.

"Bonus: You'll have more downtime with Brice," Cam clinched the request.

"Brice?" Fredo brightened maliciously. "Oh, yes, one of my brother's lackeys —"

The twins and their guardian whirled on him. "Brice Stanley?" Alex asked, shocked.

"The movie star?" Cam wanted to clarify.

"My Brice?" Ileana gulped.

"The very one," Fredo insisted, rubbing his arms and keeping an eye on Boris. "How he idolized Thantos — and obeyed him unquestioningly."

"I don't believe you," Ileana said, but Cam and Alex could see, could feel, that she did, and that Fredo's revelation had shaken her.

Cam remembered how awful it was finding out that Shane was working for Thantos. The handsome young warlock had been sent to harm them but had stayed to help. Shane had refused to kill at her cruel uncle's command. Maybe Brice Stanley, too, would disobey and abandon Lord Thantos.

"Yo, hold up," Alex insisted. "Idolized and obeyed. Past tense. How long ago did this happen, Fredo?"

"Not that long ago —"

"I don't believe you." Ileana tried to remain haughty. "Let's go. I'm transporting you home. And then I've got business — and pleasure — to take care of south of the border."

"*You're* taking me home? But you said . . ." Fredo looked pleadingly at Alex and Cam. "You said you'd come with me."

"We said," Alex reminded him, "that we wouldn't let Thantos hurt you."

"And we won't," Cam promised. "You'll have Ileana's protection, all the way back to Coventry Island."

Fredo gazed at Ileana, letting his situation sink in. "Oh, very well. Brice was just a boy," he told his traveling companion. "Very young. His parents were sick and sent him to the fortress to be reared. That was when my mother, Lady Leila, was still alive —"

"Fredo, what about our mother?" Cam asked anxiously. "Thantos said he could take us to her."

"And you believed him?" Ileana shook her head at them.

"He can and he will," Fredo declared, "if you come with me now."

Cam and Alex looked at each other, then turned to Ileana.

"She is a stranger, a nobody! I am your relative," Fredo burst out. "Would I want to hurt you?"

"You are no longer children," Ileana said stiffly. "The decision must be your own." She snapped her fingers and Boris jumped into her arms. Then she turned away from them as if preparing to leave. "Oh, all right," they heard her grumble as she swung back to face them. "I am your relative, too —"

"Who told you that?" Fredo looked around frantically. "It wasn't me. I'd never say a thing like that! Relative, ha! Not from *our* side of the family!"

Ignoring him, Cam asked softly, "Ileana, was our mother your mother, too?"

"No," their guardian said, "though I often wished she were. When I was a child, I longed for Miranda to be my mother. She was kind and beautiful. I remember growing angry with her when she told me that she and Aron were going to be parents. I became very jealous —"

"When did you see her last?" Alex asked.

"You already know. My lord Karsh told you. I saw her the day you were born. Karsh and I found your father. It was a great tragedy — for all. You see, I worshiped Lord Aron. He was brilliant and strong and his eyes were as gray as mine — and yours, of course," she added. "I dreamed that they'd adopt me one day. And Karsh told me they hoped for it, too. Who knows what might have happened. . . ."

"What did happen?" Cam urged gently. "What happened to our mother?"

"I don't know," Ileana confessed. "We brought her your father's robe, his bloodstained cloak. Lord Karsh and I stayed with her while she mourned and tore her hair. We stayed as she howled and screamed and rubbed her face into the bloody fleece of the cloak she had so lovingly made for him. We stayed and held you so that you would be safe — and, as we watched, Miranda went mad."

"A crazy woman," Fredo cackled suddenly. "That's who your mother was. Dangerously demented. Incurably insane. She needed to be locked up!"

"And my mother?!" Ileana whirled ragefully on Fredo. "What do you know of *her*?"

Fredo's pasty skin bleached to a slick and sicker white. The dark orbs of his squinty eyes darted madly, as if looking for a way out of their sockets. "W-why ask me?" he stammered. "I am not your father!"

"Who is?" Ileana demanded.

Trembling, terrified, Fredo fell to his knees in the snow. Staring defiantly at Ileana, he put his fingers to his lips and made the gesture of a key turning in a lock. "My lips are sealed," he pledged.

Ileana's hands flew up, her fingers raked the air be-

tween herself and Fredo. Her beautiful lips twisted into a snarl. There was no doubt that a terrible spell could fly from them.

"What does it matter," their uncle squealed, "whether you kill me or Thantos does?"

"No," Cam shouted.

"Ileana, don't," Alex begged. Without thinking, they dashed to her and threw their arms around her waist.

Their guardian's hands relaxed, alighting gently on the girls' heads. "Never," she whispered, stroking their hair, "would I have harmed him. I am a witch, not a demon — no matter who my father may be."

Her shoulders fell. And Boris leaped off them. Hissing and spitting, the orange cat jumped onto the foul warlock's scrawny neck.

By the time Ileana led him away, their uncle was covered in oozing hives. His eyes were swollen, his nose red. And his throat was so inflamed that he couldn't have answered another question no matter who asked it.

CHAPTER EIGHTEEN
GOING HOME

"Excellent!" Cam grinned big into her cell phone and blocked out the airport noises all around her. She listened to Bree describe the belated party her dad was finally going to throw for her. Due to some "glitch" on the set of his movie, Mr. Waxman had some unexpected time on his hands.

"It'll be the kick!" Brianna raved. "A weekend-long bash at the Boston Ritz, with major concert tickets for Saturday night. And now you can come, you'll be back from winter break."

Cam laughed. "Celebrating your fifteenth birthday is something we were always meant to do together," she said. "All of us."

A sharp pang twanged her gut. Talking to Bree led to thoughts of Beth, Sukari, Amanda, and Kristen, too. Her friends. Yes, she'd spent the last week with Alex's heart-homies. Getting to know them, helping them, had brought her closer to Lucinda and Evan. But that didn't make her miss her own BFFs any less.

Then, another eureka moment walloped her: This is what it's been like for Alex in Marble Bay. After eight months, Als was mostly cool with the Six Pack, but no one could ever replace . . .

"Wha?!" Cam yelped out loud and spun around to see Evan, who'd just lightly connected with a karate kick to her shin. On his left, Lucinda was giggling, and on his right, Alex, commanding: "Get off the horn, Barnes! Tick-tock, the plane'll be boarding and, as you would put it, 'Good-bye much?'"

Then she pinched the phone from Cam and sing-songed into it, "See ya later, Breezie-gator," adding a little more sarcastically than she'd meant to, "Oh, and BTW, thanks for including me in the invite to your party."

Cam didn't hear what Bree said next, but Alex did. As she ended the call, Brianna softly whispered, "Fly safe, you guys."

And Alex smiled in spite of herself.

"I heard your karate is way improved," Luce said, as

the foursome hustled toward the long line waiting to clear security. Lucinda gave Evan a light punch on the arm and props for his smooth moves the other night.

The boy lit up. "I never felt anything like it," he admitted, shaking his head. "It was like some generator got switched on inside me. All of a sudden there was this new power source. I guess when you get really angry," he mused, "like when someone is threatening your friends or family, you get this surge of energy, like supernatural strength, like —"

"Magick," Cam finished as Alex impulsively slipped her arm around her Raggedy-Ann-haired best, and nodded to Evan. "You really did kick butt, dude. You're a hero now — the boy who saved Crow Creek High."

Evan stuck his thumbs in the straps of his overalls and shrugged. "You guys deserve the credit. Except for a couple of choice karate moves on my part."

"Boy's head is going to get as big as his hair," Alex teased, tugging a rope of Rasta curls. Best of all, along with his threads and dreads, Evan's yummy chocolate smell was back.

The acrid burning odor, Alex realized, had probably come from his worrying so much about fire. And from holding inside what he so badly wanted to blurt.

"How's your mom doing?" Cam asked him.

"I meant to tell you." Evan grinned proudly. "I'm driving her up to rehab this afternoon. She's going to get help. I think your showing up — and everything that happened afterward — kind of gave her the push she needed." *And*, Alex heard him add strictly to himself, *she was so ashamed of not being able to help me —*

Luce laughed, but Alex said gently, "No, dude. It's because she's so proud of you. She's always wanted to be there for you and the kids."

They were next to go through the metal detector. Alex pressed her lips together and tried to push back the feelings that threatened to overwhelm her. She hugged Evan fiercely, burying her head in his chest. "Good-bye," she said, "and don't —"

"Do anything you wouldn't do?" Evan's voice was thick with emotion, too.

Cam planted a good-bye kiss on Lucinda's cheek. "You guys," Luce said as Alex moved in to give her one more hug. "I'm gonna start bawlin' if you two don't go ahead and get moving, now."

"Tell Andy my sister says 'bye,'" Alex teased, winking at Luce.

As the twins made their way to the boarding area, Cam's cell phone rang. It was Mrs. Bass. The librarian had wanted to drive them to the airport, but realized how im-

portant it was to them to say their special good-byes to Evan and Lucinda.

Apparently, she hadn't let go of something that was bothering her. She asked to speak to Alex.

"Sure." Cam shrugged and handed the phone over.

Mrs. Bass spoke quickly, in a way that made Alex realize the woman had struggled with whether or not to divulge this. And had clearly decided that if she didn't get it all out now, she never would. Alex tensed.

Signaling Cam to move closer to the phone, Alex waited nervously.

"Now that Isaac is gone," Mrs. Bass began, "I feel I really should tell you."

Alex began to feel a tightening in her stomach. What new Ike revelation was about to be dumped on her?

"I feel Sara would have wanted you to know." Mrs. Bass took a deep breath. "In fairness to the man's memory."

What had fairness to do with it? Alex thought. Where did fair ever fit into the Ike equation?

"Alex . . ." Mrs. Bass paused. "Isaac didn't walk out on you and Sara."

Alex laughed. "Right. He *ran* out."

"He begged to stay, but your mother had made up her mind. She kicked him out," Doris continued.

"Because he was a gambler, a loser, a . . ." Alex ticked off the reasons. What was the difference?

"She never told me why," Mrs. Bass explained, "but knowing Sara as well as I did . . . it had to be something pretty monumental. She'd always intended for you to be brought up with two parents. But something made her change her mind."

In the background, Alex and Cam could hear the announcement that their plane was boarding.

"I just thought you should know," Mrs. Bass said.

Alex's spiked head rested against the plane's window, her gaze fixed on the tweedy pattern of the seat back in front of her. She listened to but didn't look directly at Cam in the aisle seat next to her.

"Why do you think Mrs. Bass decided to drop that little detail now?" Cam didn't have to read Alex's mind to know her sister was obsessing about that last phone call.

"What's to think about?" Alex responded glumly. "She obviously had this need to go all 'truth, justice, and the librarian way.' My mom told me Ike bailed. Bass says no, Sara sent him packing. It changes nothing."

"And just leads to more questions that may never be answered," Cam finished the thought for her twin.

"Speaking of." Alex flexed in her seat, intent on

changing the subject. "Our guardian's got a few issues of her own in search of answers. Like the famous Brice Stanley — warlock, movie star, Ileana crush-puppy, and tool of Thantos?!"

Cam shuddered, remembering Shane. "I feel her pain, I really do."

Alex considered. "You'd think the brilliant Ileana would have sensed that Brice was hooked up with our murderous uncle."

"Maybe love dulls our senses? She's so into him. But if anyone can figure it out, Ileana can. That's our . . . what? Cousin, aunt, random relative, guardian?"

"That's our goddess," Alex declared, laughing — knowing, as Cam did, that the truth, whatever it turned out to be, wouldn't hide from Ileana for long. The most talented and tyrannical witch they knew would simply not allow it to.

Alex had no clue how long she'd slept. What she did know was: The plane was in the air, en route from Montana to Massachusetts. It hadn't stopped. Yet someone had gotten aboard who hadn't been there before.

And, though she'd awakened smiling, a tear was running down her cheek.

Someone had visited her — the same pale and gentle, raspy-voiced old man who'd been tapping into her

dreams, talking to her, guiding her, for as long as she could remember.

Karsh.

The ancient warlock hadn't sneaked into her slumber in quite a while. Today he'd returned, as real to her as the sleeve of the plaid flannel shirt on which she was now wiping her tears. And this time, this visit, she'd been able to talk to him.

"Child," he'd said soothingly, "let me ease your struggle."

And she remembered saying, "If Mrs. Bass knew that Sara kicked Ike out, why'd she wait until he was dead to tell me?"

"Ah, Artemis, surely you must know. As long as Isaac Fielding was alive, he was a threat to you. Your protector, Sara, discovered that. The librarian merely did what Sara wanted: promote the idea that Isaac chose to leave."

"But wasn't he a loser, a gambler, a creep? Didn't he steal all our money? Why else would she have thrown him out? Why would she have chosen to live in poverty?"

"He did take the money," Karsh assured her. "He was furious that she wanted him out; his pride was wounded . . . enough to vengefully make off with Sara's savings. But he wasn't all bad, Artemis. No one is all bad — or all good. Isaac Fielding had many faults. The gambling, an illness, was one of them. But when he

wasn't sick, he worked. And he brought in enough money to keep Sara and you sheltered, clothed and fed."

"Did she love him?" Alex heard herself asking weakly.

"She did, my child, she did. She would have put up with his vanity, problems, and get-rich schemes . . . until it happened."

Whatever had happened, Alex knew, was the reason Sara turned her back on Ike. "It had to do with me, didn't it? You have to tell me what it was."

Karsh smiled — at her quickness, her cleverness, Alex sensed — and then he confirmed her gut feeling. "Isaac saw you do something . . . remarkable. You didn't realize what you'd done. You were merely a child, a cranky, overtired little girl having a temper tantrum in a store. You wanted a small, silly, but extraordinarily expensive doll. Sara correctly said no. Yet somehow the doll ended up in the shopping cart at the checkout counter.

"Isaac had seen you staring at the toy but knew you hadn't touched it. He had seen something with no rational explanation. His greed and scheming took over. He wanted to test you, to see if you could do it again, to train you. To see if he could make money —"

"— illegally, by stealing stuff?" Alex was stunned, repulsed.

Karsh had nodded then, sadly. "Sara was appalled.

Her husband's true colors had come out, and she knew she could never again trust him to be around you. There was really no decision to be made."

"So she cut him loose," Alex concluded.

"She chose to work two jobs, to be a single mother. And she chose to tell you only about one side of the man. The dark side. She wanted to be sure that even after she was gone, you would never seek him out."

Alex understood. Sara had chosen poverty over comfort, being alone over love, possibly even death over life. The cigarette smoking that led to her lung cancer had probably been fueled by stress as well as nicotine.

"All to protect me," Alex marveled aloud.

"That was her destiny. She was your protector, Artemis. That is why I chose her."

Now Alex was awake. Karsh was gone. Sniffing back a final tear, Alex turned to Cam, eager to share the old warlock's revelations.

But her sister's seat was empty.

While Alex had dozed, Cam had tried to read, to listen to music, to watch the movie she'd already seen at the multiplex, but nothing could distract her.

As we watched, Miranda went mad, she kept hearing Ileana say. And then Fredo's vicious voice piping up: *She deserved to be locked up!*

Nothing seemed to happen by accident in her world,

not since she and Alex had found each other. So what did it mean, what was she supposed to do with these stunning discoveries?

Slowly, methodically, Cam tried to put the pieces together to remember everything they'd been told about their mother. Her name was Miranda. She was kind, adored, beautiful, and wildly — or was it madly, Cam sorrowfully wondered — in love with their father. Miranda had found the perfect partner in Aron, the brilliant gray-eyed young warlock who, the newspaper had said, was the founder of a "multimillion-dollar technology empire" — that their uncle now headed. She had lost Aron the very day Cam and Alex were born. Karsh and Ileana had found him and brought Miranda his lambs-wool cloak. And their mother's grief had turned to madness. Now she was gone, vanished. Neither Karsh nor Ileana knew her fate. They assumed Miranda was dead, lost forever to those who loved her.

Only Thantos acted differently. Their villainous uncle insisted he could take the twins to Miranda. Which didn't mean Miranda was alive, Cam had to remind herself. Either the evil snake meant he could take them to her grave — or he could summon up her spirit. She and Alex had accidentally brought the spirit of their grandmother, Leila, to the sacred stream. No doubt that's what the deceitful Thantos meant.

The more Cam pondered, the surer she became. That had to be it. If Miranda were alive, she would have come looking for them.

And yet, no one had ever said for sure that she was dead. Her body had never been found.

Even under the fleece airline blanket, Cam had become chilled. Her sight had grown blurry and her head began to ache. Probably from thinking too much, she tried to tell herself. But all at once, a vision she'd had — when was it? months ago — came flying back at her like a boomerang.

Blinding brightness. A woman bathed in white light. A long chestnut braid down her back. Staring, watching, waiting . . .

The light, the brightness? The woman had been looking out a big window, as if inside a greenhouse.

"Put the pieces together, Apolla. You can do it. You must do it. It is your destiny."

The voice, Karsh's raspy whisper, had invaded her vision then. Or was it a vision? No, she had fallen asleep after all. And their guardian's guardian, the faithful old warlock who had known and loved her parents, had come to her. Not to answer her questions but to guide her in using her own powers. He had come to urge her once again to trust her premonitions.

It was then that Cam had gotten up to stretch her legs. As she walked back to her seat now, she saw Alex

popping up, looking around for her. Before she could say anything, Alex said, "Karsh came to me. I know why Sara kicked out Ike."

Cam let her sister explain and put her arm around Alex. "Sara was really heroic, Als. You knew that."

"I just never knew how heroic," Alex admitted, so relieved and grateful to have Cam to share everything with. She had so many mixed emotions. And Cam understood them all.

"Apparently," Cam was saying, "I snoozed, too — and had a little visit from Karsh."

"He told you about Sara?" Alex asked excitedly.

"No, it was all topic Miranda. I don't think Karsh knows our mother's fate, but he told me to 'put the pieces together.'"

"And?"

Cam took a deep breath and recounted every fact, and what she now believed her vision meant.

Alex finished the thought: "That picture of Thantos outside that 'clinic,' that sanatorium. What if he wasn't there as a patient, but as a visitor?"

Wherever that picture had been taken, wherever that institution was, that's where their mother might be — sick, or even desperately insane, but alive!

They didn't say it aloud. They didn't have to. They were two with one thought.

"We're beginning our initial descent into the Boston area." Coming through the sound system, the flight attendant's voice jarred them. "Please fasten your seat belts, stow your tray tables, and bring your seat backs to the upright position."

Alex smiled suddenly and looked out the window. The lights of Boston twinkled below. "Home sweet home," she said to Cam.

"I wasn't sure whether you considered it home yet," Cam admitted, smiling sheepishly.

"I don't," her sister said.

Cam's smile faded. "Then it's still Montana?"

"Montana, Massachusetts, Coventry Island — Sister T*Witch," Alex said, "wherever we're together, that's home."

ABOUT THE AUTHORS

H.B. Gilmour is the author of numerous best-selling books for adults and young readers, including the *Clueless* movie novelization and series; *Pretty in Pink,* a University of Iowa Best Book for Young Readers; and *Godzilla,* a Nickelodeon Kids Choice nominee. She also cowrote the award-winning screenplay *Tag*.

H.B. lives in upstate New York with her husband, John Johann, and their puppy Harrison, one of the family's five dogs, four cats, two snakes (a boa constrictor and a python), and five extremely bright, animal-loving children.

Randi Reisfeld has written many best-sellers, such as the *Clueless* series (which she wrote with H.B.); the *Moesha* series; and biographies of Prince William, New Kids on the Block, and Hanson. Her Scholastic paperback *Got Issues Much?* was named an ALA Best Book for Reluctant Readers in 1999.

Randi has always been fascinated with the randomness of life. . . . About how any of our lives can simply "turn on a dime" and instantly (*snap!*) be forever changed. About the power each one of us has deep inside, if only we knew how to access it. About how any of us would react if, out of the blue, we came face-to-face with our exact double.

From those random fascinations, T*Witches was born.

Oh, and BTW: She has no twin (that she knows of) but an extremely cool family and cadre of BFFs to whom she is totally devoted.

They're Twins. They're Witches.

T•WITCHES

They're identically powerful—
yet radically different.

And they didn't know
each other existed
...until now.

Get inside the head of your favorite T*WITCH.
Visit each sister's desktop at

www.scholastic.com/twitches

❏ BGG 0-439-24070-0	T*Witches #1: The Power of Two	$4.50
❏ BGG 0-439-24071-9	T*Witches #2: Building a Mystery	$4.50
❏ BGG 0-439-24072-7	T*Witches #3: Seeing Is Deceiving	$4.50
❏ BGG 0-439-24073-5	T*Witches #4: Dead Wrong	$4.50

Available wherever you buy books, or use this order form.

Scholastic Inc., P.O. Box 7502, Jefferson City, MO 65102

Please send me the books I have checked above. I am enclosing $_____ (please add $2.00 to cover shipping and handling). Send check or money order—no cash or C.O.D.s please.

Name_____Birth date_____

Address_____

City_____State/Zip_____

Please allow four to six weeks for delivery. Offer good in U.S.A. only. Sorry, mail orders are not available to residents of Canada. Prices subject to change.

📖 SCHOLASTIC   TW4